ROOSEVELT GRADY

ROOSEVELT GRADY

LOUISA R. SHOTWELL

Illustrated by Peter Burchard

THE WORLD PUBLISHING COMPANY

CLEVELAND AND NEW YORK

Published by The World Publishing Company
2231 West 110th Street, Cleveland 2, Ohio
Published simultaneously in Canada by
Nelson, Foster & Scott Ltd.
Library of Congress Catalog Card Number: 63-14778
First Edition
COWP

To Edith Lowry

CONTENTS

ROOSEVELT GRADY

Taking Away

The Opportunity Class. That's where the bean-pickers got put.

Roosevelt Grady wondered what it meant.

Roosevelt knew about schools. Third grade, fourth grade, things like that. He knew about schools from experience: three weeks here, six weeks there, a day or two somewhere else. But Opportunity Class. This was something new.

Looking around the schoolroom, he decided that Opportunity Class must mean mixing up the little children and the big boys and girls in the same room. But why? Opportunity for what?

The teacher was Miss Gladys. She wore a black dress all wrinkles and chalk dust. She was skin and bones strung together; no soft fat places anywhere. She had a voice like the horn on Cap Jackson's beat-up truck, trembly but plenty loud. She taught with a stick.

The children sang. You couldn't hear anybody but Miss Gladys. Her horny voice drowned out the sound of everybody else. Roosevelt couldn't even hear himself, but he kept on singing anyway.

The stick jerked back and forth on each beat.

"Look away" (*jerk jerk*)
"Look away" (*jerk jerk*)
"Look away" (*jerk jerk*)
"Dixie Land" (*jerk jerk*)

In oral reading, *tap tap tap* went the stick on the blackboard, three taps for every word.

Two girls fell to giggling. Miss Gladys held the stick straight up in the air and high. It worked like magic. The room got still as a piney wood. One thing was plain. Nobody wanted a licking.

Time came for figures.

Roosevelt looked at his work sheet. A whole page full of nothing but taking away.

Take 12 from 17. A cinch. He licked his stubby pencil and in the answer space he wrote a nice fat 5.

Take 28 from 33. Same old answer. He began to get bored. He made another fat 5 and this time he put a curly tail on it.

Take 29 from 84. Here was a mean one, but it

didn't catch Roosevelt. He knew all about taking away. This answer had to be 55.

Miss Gladys must be crazy about 5's.

Roosevelt was sick and tired of 5's.

He was sick and tired of taking away. He wanted to learn about putting into.

At the last school where he'd been, they'd finished taking away and begun on putting into. That he liked. Being there when they began on something new made him feel regular, as though he belonged.

Besides, putting into had one special thing about it he purely had to find out.

So here he was in a new school, all ready to learn more about putting into and not a thing to work on but the same old taking away.

He sighed. He went back and added curly tails to the 55, bottom and top.

The boy behind him tapped on his shoulder and whispered: "What's that you're making?"

Roosevelt covered his paper with both hands and didn't answer.

The boy made a dive for the paper. In nothing flat the two of them were in the aisle, wrestling.

Crack! Smack down on their two heads came Miss Gladys' stick.

"We don't have nonsense here," she announced.

The boys slunk back into their seats and rubbed their heads.

Miss Gladys went on. "Here we never forget," she said. "We are the Opportunity Class."

That was when Roosevelt said it. He had no idea he was going to speak, but he did.

"Please, ma'am," he asked, "opportunity for what?"

Silence.

Somebody tittered and all at once the whole class burst out laughing. They roared and they rocked in their seats. The boys thumped each other. The girls poked their elbows into their neighbors' ribs and shrieked with delight.

Shame burned inside Roosevelt's head and his eyes smarted. He hadn't meant to be funny or fresh or anything. He simply wanted to know.

Up in the air went the stick and they all got quiet.

"Exactly what, young man," said Miss Gladys, "do you want opportunity for?"

Roosevelt felt miserable but he couldn't see any way to back down. "For putting into," he said. "Please, ma'am, I want opportunity to learn about putting into."

Miss Gladys stared at him.

He plunged on. "I'm tired of taking away," he explained desperately. "There's a thing I need to know about putting into."

Another silence.

Then came the surprise of the day. Roosevelt

couldn't believe his ears. Miss Gladys giggled. And
then she began laughing so hard she dropped the
stick. She had to go and sit down behind her desk.
She opened a drawer and took out a white handker-
chief. She wiped her eyes and then she blew her nose,
loud.

"Hands up," she said, "all those who are tired of
taking away."

All over the room hands shot up.

"Hands up," she said, "all those who want to learn
about putting into."

Again the air shivered with waving hands.

"Very well. Tomorrow," she said, "tomorrow all

the big boys and girls will study putting into. That's a promise."

Roosevelt felt good. As if he belonged.

After school, the boy who'd grabbed for his paper stopped him on the way to the bus. For the first time Roosevelt had a good look at his wrestling mate. He was a big boy, a good two sizes bigger than Roosevelt. He had on a corduroy jacket, bright green.

"Take it easy, man," he said. "Be seeing you." And he loped off.

On the bus Roosevelt looked around, but the green jacket was nowhere in sight. To the boy in the seat beside him, he said: "Who was that kid? The one I tangled in the aisle with."

"Oh, him? He's Digger Burton's handy-boy. Name's Manowar."

"Manowar what?" asked Roosevelt.

"Nothing. Just Manowar."

As the bus rolled along beside the irrigation ditch, Roosevelt sank down into the cushy seat low on his spine and shut his eyes. Manowar. What a name! He wished he had an older brother like that.

Then he thought about putting into. About that special thing he wanted to know. Tomorrow he'd find out. Miss Gladys would explain it. Maybe she wasn't such a bad teacher, after all, even if she did have a voice like a trembly truck horn. Even if she did teach with a stick. Maybe the Opportunity Class was a good place for bean-pickers. A place where they could find out things. If they asked.

Back home in camp came the second surprise of the day, and this was not a good surprise. The Grady family was packing up.

"Beans all run out," said his father. "Nothing more to pick here. We'll pull out early in the morning. Head north."

Roosevelt's heart dropped. Here it was happening all over again. Not ever, probably, would he get to stay put in a school long enough so he'd really belong.

Putting Into

Roosevelt bunched his sweater underneath him to soften the jouncing floor of the moving truck. He leaned his head back against his mother's arm. If the air got any chillier, he'd have to take his sweater out from under him and put it on to keep warm, but it wasn't quite that cold. Not yet.

Along with three other families, the Gradys rode in the back of the truck. All but Papa, who sat up front to spell Cap Jackson. Cap was the regular driver and he was the crew leader, too. He owned the truck and in it he carried the people to places where crops were ready for picking.

"We're heading for beans and cucumbers," Cap Jackson said.

Roosevelt's mother sat straight up on the flat side of the family suitcase. It was made of metal and it was slippery, so she had her feet planted wide apart and flat on the floor to brace herself. On her lap she held Princess Anne, sleeping.

Between Mamma's feet lay Sister. She was seven years old and dainty, with dimples. Her smile, Papa always said, could charm a snake out of a tree.

"Honest, could it?" Roosevelt asked him once.

"Well, I tell you, Roosevelt," Papa said, "the first time we find a snake in a tree, we'll get Sister to smile at him and we'll see what happens." So far they hadn't found a tree with a snake in it.

On the other side of Mamma slumped Matthew, who was only five and chubby. Matthew had a lame foot, but that didn't keep him from enjoying life. He was great on making jokes, and he didn't miss a thing.

The truck had a canvas roof. The roof sloped up on each side to a peak like the top of a barn, and it kept you from seeing the sky. Anyway, it was dark outside. It was the middle of the night, but the truck kept right on going.

Between sleeping and waking, Roosevelt thought about putting into. He thought about that special thing he wanted to know. The question kept running around his head the way a mosquito teases you in the dark.

This was his question: When you put something into something else and it doesn't come out even, what do you do with what's left over?

What happened yesterday was exactly what had happened at the school where he'd first heard about putting into. The teacher came to where it seemed she must explain it the very next day. And then what? That time it wasn't beans that ran out. It was celery, but it didn't matter what the crop was. If it ran out, it ran out, and that was the end. The whole family packed up and piled into Cap Jackson's sputtery old truck and away they went to find a place where onions or tomatoes or some old thing was coming along ready to harvest. And same as yesterday, Roosevelt never got back to school to hear what the teacher had to say.

Some places there wouldn't be any school at all. Or else there'd be a school and the bean-picker boys and girls didn't get to go to it. The school would be for residents, and bean-picker families weren't residents. They didn't belong.

Once there was a school and it was closed when they got there. It was closed because the crop was ripe. A crop vacation, folks called this, and everybody picked, young ones and grown-ups and old people. Everybody except, of course, Princess Anne. Over in Louisiana she sat by herself in a fruit crate at the end of the strawberry rows and sucked her thumb, cute as a bug.

Roosevelt rubbed his eyes, leaned his head against Mamma's knee, and tried hard to go to sleep. He'd almost made it when buzz went that old mosquito

again, nagging at him about putting into. Like 3 into
17. You can't say 17's got six 3's in it, because six 3's
need 18. So the answer has to be five 3's. But that's
only 15. So what do you do with the poor little 2 that
gets left over?

Roosevelt liked to have things come out even. He
liked to have a place to put every piece of whatever
it was he had. He liked to pick all the ripe beans quick
and clean off one plant and then move along that row
to the next. He liked to fill his basket just full enough
so it was even across the top. If one bean stuck up in
the air, he'd pull it out and make a little hole among
the other beans and poke it carefully down in. He
liked to make a pan of corn bread and cut it into
exactly enough squares to make one piece for everybody in the family. Except Princess Anne. Her teeth
hadn't come through far enough yet to chew anything
crusty. Sometimes Mamma would break off a little
of her piece of corn bread and dunk it in her coffee to
soften it. Then she gave that to Princess Anne.

Bouncing along through the dark, Roosevelt got to
thinking some more about numbers. Take nine. Right
now nine was an important number in his life. He
was nine years old. His birthday was the ninth day
of September, and if you began to count the months
with January one and February two and so on, what
did September turn out to be? Why, nine!

To be perfectly sure, he whispered the months over

to himself, counting on his fingers. Sure enough, nine came out to be September.

How many different schools had he been to in his lifetime? He counted to himself. Six, seven, eight . . . and nine. There was that nine again. Different schools, that is. If you counted twice the schools he'd been to and then gone back to, they made thirteen, but Roosevelt didn't want to count that way. He didn't like the number thirteen. Papa said thirteen was unlucky. Mamma said she didn't believe in lucky or unlucky, but there was no use tempting fate.

"What's tempting fate?" Roosevelt asked her.

"It means trying to outsmart the devil," Mamma said. "And he's really smart. You're best off to stay clean away from thirteen this and thirteen that. You can just as easy make it twelve or fourteen and not take any chances."

One day a while back, Roosevelt had asked Papa about putting into and the poor little leftover number. He had laughed and said: "Just throw it away."

But Roosevelt couldn't feel right doing that. What would become of it?

Another day he had asked Mamma. She said: "Save it till you need it."

"What do you do with it," Roosevelt wanted to know, "while you're waiting to need it?"

Mamma didn't laugh nearly so often as Papa did, but she laughed that time.

"Put it in your pocket," she said, "and go fetch me a bucket of water."

The Secret

The truck jerked to a stop, and the motor coughed and went still. From the driver's seat, Cap Jackson called out:

"Anybody want a drink? There's a spring here at the edge of the woods."

The people stirred. Cap came around and let down the tailgate and put up the ladder. Roosevelt experimented with a swallow and his mouth felt dry, so he clambered down. The stars were bright. The air was cold and it had a piney smell, clean and fresh. He waited his turn in line in front of a pipe with water bubbling out of it. In the starlight the pipe looked rusty. The men had to stoop over to reach it, but it was exactly the right height for Roosevelt. He didn't have to bend down or stand on his toes, either one.

When his turn came, the water was cool and he took a big gulp, but it didn't taste good. Not good at all. It tasted like a bad egg.

"Sulphur water," said one of the men.

Roosevelt spit his mouthful out on the ground. He shivered. When he climbed back into the truck, he put his sweater on and sat right flat down on the boards.

As the motor wheezed and the truck began to move, Sister and Matthew both woke up and wiggled. Roosevelt was glad they'd waked up. He felt like having company.

"Talk to us, Mamma," said Matthew. "Tell us a story."

"Hush," said Mamma. "Other folks want to go to sleep."

"Talk to us soft-like," begged Matthew. "Whisper to us about . . . you know . . ."

Roosevelt knew what was coming. Matthew always asked for the same story. It was Roosevelt's favorite story, too.

". . . about the olden days. And the dog run."

"All right," said Mamma. "Lean close and I'll tell it to you short. Then you go to sleep."

And she did. She didn't make it too short either. About the little house in the cotton field in Georgia, how it sat up on stilts and was a house in two parts like, with this comfortable sitting-out place in be-

tween and a roof over the whole thing. The sitting-
out place was the dog run, and it had a rocking chair
like President Kennedy's.

The Gradys had a dog there too, a hound, sort of.
Named Nellie. She had short tan hair and floppy ears
and brown eyes. Her eyes were wistful.

"What's wistful?" Matthew demanded.

"Wistful is you want something and you don't
know what," said Mamma.

They had chickens, too, and two big pigs and a
litter of little pigs. And a goat. And growing out back
they had sweet potatoes and collards and mustard
greens.

Roosevelt moved his tongue around to see if he
could make himself remember the taste of a sweet
potato. He couldn't.

Now it was Sister's turn. Was she still awake? She
was.

"Take us back to your wedding day, Mamma,"
she said. "Tell us about your white dress and what
Papa said."

"There was this magnolia tree," said Mamma,
"right outside the Pink Lily Baptist Church. And it
was brim full of waxy white blossoms. I wore a shiny
white dress with a green sash and long streamers and
I had a veil, all cloudy, made of net. Your papa told
me I was almost the prettiest thing in the whole
county.

" '*Almost* the prettiest? Why *almost*?' I said, kind of sniffy and jealous."

"Jealous," said Sister. "Tell us what's jealous."

"Jealous is you're scared somebody you like likes somebody else better than you," Mamma explained. "Now don't interrupt me any more. And your papa said, 'You or that magnolia tree. I can't make up my mind which one is prettier. But I'll pick you.' So off we went to live in the little house in the cotton field."

"Now tell us why we left the little house in the cotton field," insisted Matthew. "Why did we go away and leave our dog Nellie and the little pigs and the dog run all behind us?"

"Why we left? Why, honey, the machines came along. The tractors got bigger and bigger and they did more and more of the work the people used to do. Mr. Wilson let us stay on a while and your papa got some work in the sawmill six miles off. But pretty soon Mr. Wilson plain had to tear down our house to plant more cotton. So that's when we went on the season, looking for work wherever we could find it."

She stopped a minute. When she went on, her voice sounded different. Angry, almost.

"Some folks say now they've even got a machine that knows how to pick cotton. A big red monster. With fingers."

Sister sighed, a long whishy sigh that meant she

was on her way to sleep again. Roosevelt waited. When Matthew breathed so even it seemed certain he must be asleep too, Roosevelt sat up close to Mamma's ear.

"Now let's you and me talk about our secret," he whispered.

"Hush," said Mamma.

"Please," said Roosevelt.

Mamma didn't say anything right away, and Roosevelt sat stiff and still. Then she spoke, not whispering but still so low he could hardly hear. She said just what he knew she'd say.

"Someday we'll find ourselves a house in a place where there's work for your papa every one of all twelve months in the year. Maybe the house won't have a dog run, but it'll sure enough be a home. And you and Sister and Matthew will go to school, the same school right along, day in, day out, fall and winter and right on to the end of spring."

"And Princess Anne?" asked Roosevelt.

"Princess Anne, too, soon as she's big enough. You'll all go right along with the children that belong. Because we'll be in a place where we'll all belong. We'll be right out of this bean-picking rat race and we'll stay put."

"How will we find this place?" asked Roosevelt anxiously, even though he'd asked this before and knew what the answer would be.

"I don't know how," said Mamma, "but we'll know it when we see it. There'll be something about it so we'll know it. And don't you forget. This is our secret."

"It's our secret," said Roosevelt, and he dropped his head in the crook of Mamma's elbow and fell sound asleep.

The Great Bay

All next day and through the whole of the second night they trundled on. Early the following morning Cap Jackson drove the truck right onto a big boat.

"We're crossing the great bay," said Papa. "Pretty soon we'll get to the camp on the Eastern Shore." Papa was riding in the back now. "This is a ferryboat."

Sister squealed. "A fairyboat! Where do they keep the fairies? I want to see one."

"Sister, if you went all over this boat from top to bottom and stem to stern, you wouldn't find one fairy half so pretty as Delois Grady," Papa told her. Delois. That was Sister's real name.

Mamma said, "Henry, you're spoiling that child." Papa laughed and tickled Sister in the stomach. She squealed again. It was true she was pretty, and you

could hardly blame Papa for saying so. If only she
didn't squeal so much. Probably she couldn't help it.
After all, she was just a girl.

Sister couldn't go looking for a fairy, and nobody
could see what the water looked like in the bay because they had to stay right in the truck the whole
time.

"The pilot can't have kids running all over the
boat," Cap Jackson told them. "You can understand
that."

This was the way it always was, traveling from crop
to crop. You never got a chance to see anything in

between. It would be fun, just once sometime, to stop off somewhere and see something.

For breakfast Mamma gave them bread and bologna and potato chips and root beer. All of it was left over from what Papa had bought at a roadside stand the night before. The potato chips were rubbery and the root beer was warm. Cap Jackson bought some cold milk for Princess Anne.

It wasn't long after they left the ferryboat till they turned off the highway, rattled along a bumpy road, turned again over a short little thundery loose-boarded bridge, and came to a halt. This must be the camp.

Roosevelt stood up and peered over the tailgate, but all he saw was the little old bridge and a tiny stream and a bean field.

Quimby's Quarters

This camp wasn't a camp exactly. That is, it didn't look like any camp they'd come to before. It was a house.

A house might be a place you could stay put in.

The house had a name. Cap Jackson told it to them. "Its name is Quimby's Quarters," he said. "Mr. Quimby owns it."

It was a big wooden house, wide and tall, and it had a porch across the front and along one side. The porch railing and the under edges of the roof were decorated with curlycues cut out of wood.

"Look," Roosevelt said to Sister. "Mr. Quimby or somebody must have liked this house a lot."

"How do you know?" Sister asked.

"Why, look at those curlycues," Roosevelt explained. "Those are hard to make. They take a long time. Mr. Quimby must have set store by this house to put all that work on it."

"Roosevelt," said Matthew, "suppose somebody asked you what color this house is. What would you say?"

Roosevelt looked at the house. The outside walls had patchy remainders of paint on them, mustardy-colored but old-looking.

"I don't think anybody's going to ask you that, Matthew," he said, "but if somebody does, you'll do right if you say it's a rather tan house."

"Tan like our dog Nellie?" said Matthew. "It's a Nellie-color, that's what color it is."

Somebody squealed. Sister, of course. "They're expecting us," she said.

The front door did hang wide open, looking as if it was waiting for people to come inside.

On the first floor there were four rooms, all full of people. Different families were living in each room.

They trooped upstairs and here were four more rooms. These were empty. Other families from Cap Jackson's crew took three of these rooms, and Cap Jackson himself and his family took the fourth room. So up some more stairs the Gradys went.

By this time Roosevelt had about decided this couldn't be the stay-put place he and his mother had in mind. What would a family with only four children in it do with a house that had eight rooms and more besides?

The third floor turned out to be all one big room. "It's the attic," said Papa.

Roosevelt had never been in an attic before. He'd never even heard of such a place.

"What's an attic?" asked Matthew. Wouldn't you know he'd ask? If he'd just look around, he'd see what it was. But he had to ask—ask—ask.

Roosevelt was glad the attic was the only living space left for the Gradys. It was big and shadowy and its roof sloped down low on all four sides. There was only one spot where Papa could stand up straight. That spot was right in the middle. Papa was tall. Most places in that attic even a nine-year-old could easily bump his head.

Matthew thought this was great. Of course he was only five and short, but right away he began limping along the wall, and every couple of steps he'd stop and stand on the tiptoe of his one good foot and stretch his neck up till his head touched the slanty roof and then he'd say: "Ouch! Who hit me? Roosevelt, you stop that!"

The first time he said it, Roosevelt started to answer back. Then he saw that Matthew was teasing him. This was just one of old Matthew's jokes. He had such a good time making them, you couldn't stay sore at him more than a minute.

Cut right into the roof and sitting side by side like triplets were three baby windows.

"Dormer windows, folks call those," said Papa. He knew everything about houses.

Mamma brushed away the cobwebs and the dust with her hand, but the panes were still smeary. Even so, you could look across the bean fields and some woods and way over, it seemed, into the next county. Maybe when the windows got cleaner, you could see right onto that great bay they never did get a look at. If the glass ever got clean as clean, what was to keep you from looking down to Georgia, where they lived long ago when Roosevelt was only five years old?

"Those dormer windows give our attic a real glory," Mamma declared.

Before long Roosevelt decided the attic had another glory too. There was a separate sleeping place for everybody in the family! You might say it had six beds, even one for Princess Anne. Her bed was actually an old trunk with a tray in the top, but she fell right to sleep in the tray and straightway it turned into a bed.

Matthew's bed was a leather chest with a rounded bottom that just fitted his plump curves.

Sister looked inside the chest and made an awful face. "It smells of dirty clothes and fish," she said.

Matthew wrinkled up his nose and sniffed and he

said: "It's a satisfac-tory smell. I like it." He'd just learned to say satisfactory and he used it all the time.

For Sister, Mamma pulled a drawer right out of a big old bureau she found in a corner and Sister curled up in the drawer. Mamma and Papa each had a cot.

But the best bed of all was Roosevelt's. It was a hammock. It hung from the rafters. This was the first time Roosevelt could ever remember sleeping all by himself. He could kick his legs and swing the hammock and nobody cared. He liked it.

Roosevelt in Charge

The beans here weren't ready yet, Cap Jackson said, but a few miles west there might be cucumbers.

Next morning before sunup, probably about six o'clock or maybe even five, Mamma and Papa went off somewhere west in the truck to find the cucumbers.

It was a lot later than six when Roosevelt woke up and found his folks gone, but he didn't worry. He knew why they weren't there and he knew what to do. He was used to being left in charge.

From the night before, he knew how to get water. You took the bucket and went down the two flights of stairs and outdoors to a pump in the yard. So he went.

Climbing back up to the attic, he jiggled the

bucket a couple of times by accident and spilled a little water but not very much.

Everywhere they went, Mamma's oil stove traveled with them. Roosevelt got the stove going and put coffee and hominy grits to cooking for breakfast. He mixed up some powdered milk and water in Princess Anne's bottle and put a little of the coffee in it. He looked in the trunk, and there was Princess Anne awake and making gurgly noises to herself. He gave her the bottle and she went right to work on it. She was a good feeder.

Then he woke up Matthew and Sister and made them get up. This took a little doing. Roosevelt and Sister used water from the bucket to wash themselves. They both liked to feel clean. Matthew wouldn't wash.

"When I stay dirty," he announced, "I feel more satisfac-tory." He only said this partly to give himself a chance to say that word and partly because he plain hated to wash. He never washed except when Mamma was right there making him. Even then he had a pure genius for thinking up reasons for not washing. This morning the reason was good. Roosevelt did admit that.

"You and Sister used up all the clean water," Matthew argued. "So I can't wash. Good!"

Along with the oil stove, another thing that always

traveled with them was the washtub. It was the color
of silver, and handier than a suitcase, Mamma said,
for packing overflow stuff.

"You can go on outdoors and play," said Roosevelt
to Sister and Matthew.

Then he lugged the empty washtub down to the
first floor, pushed it bumpety-bump down the porch
steps, and set it on the ground underneath an oak
tree. The tree had some dark red cut-out dried-up
leaves on it left over from the fall, and new little
pinkish fluffs coming on for spring.

He went back up to the attic and lifted Princess
Anne out of the trunk. She fastened her arms tight
around his neck and he carried her downstairs and
outdoors and set her in the washtub. It made a fine
play pen. She crowed.

Roosevelt took a look around. There were children
all over the yard, but every one of them looked
smaller than nine years old.

There were three boys who kept climbing up on
the porch railing, standing up on it, and then jump-
ing to the ground. Most times they fell down. Roosevelt didn't feel like doing that. Two other boys were
trying to shinny up the oak tree and having no luck.
The branches were too high, but they kept trying.
Roosevelt didn't want to do that either. He wished
he had somebody his own size to play with or maybe
a little bigger. Even then he'd wait to find out if he

liked the boy and the boy liked him. Then they'd say a few words to each other and after a while they'd go fishing. That's what Roosevelt enjoyed best. Fishing. Either by himself or with another boy who didn't talk too much.

Sister and Matthew were always wanting plenty of kids to play with. They ought to like it here. Sister was standing near the porch now, looking down at some girls underneath it. One of them peeked out at her.

"Hi," said the peeker. "What's your name?"

"Delois," Sister said. "Delois-Grady-but-everybody-calls-me-Sister." She always explained it fast like that. "What's yours?"

"Mine's Becky," the girl called back from underneath the porch, "but I'm playing Mrs. Brown. You can play too if you want to."

"Who can I be?" asked Sister.

"Well, we need somebody for the Welfare Lady. You could be her, I guess."

"How do I be her?" Sister wanted to know.

"You pretend like to knock on the door. Then you come in all snoopy and la-di-da and ask a lot of questions."

So Sister knocked on the door and then she crawled underneath the porch.

Girls, thought Roosevelt. They sure can get busy at the funniest things. Snoopy and la-di-da. Weird.

His eyes wandered over beyond the washtub and the oak tree and the pump and onto a big heap of rubbish—inner tubes and bedspring coils and old frying pans and the insides of somebody's radio and a stovepipe and pieces of mattress with straw busting out—all charred, the pieces were, as if the mattress had started to burn and got snuffed out. There were all these things in a jumble, and right in the middle of this junk was old Matthew, crawling around and grubbing to see what he could find. He'd find something, for sure; he always did.

It looked as though everybody else was fixed for

a while. Roosevelt twisted slowly on one foot till he stood with his back to the house, facing the loose-boarded bridge the truck had thundered over last night riding them into Quimby's Quarters. Right away he knew what he'd do. He'd explore. He'd follow the brook under the bridge and see where it went. He'd see if it had any fish in it.

He took a look at Princess Anne in the washtub. She was sucking her thumb and seemed halfway to sleep. So off he went.

The brook wasn't deep and it had a soft bottom with here and there a few stones. He rolled up the legs of his jeans. The water felt good around his ankles, and the sweet wet sand oozed between his toes. He followed the brook along between the bean fields and pretty soon it led him into woods. The water got deeper, but still he saw no real fish, only a shiner or two, so he climbed out and did some exploring in among the trees.

Here the sun felt far away. Some of the trees had white flowers on them. Shad bush, that was. Some had reddish-purple flowers just beginning to open. Judas trees, like in the Bible. Mamma said folks called them that because you couldn't tell were they red or were they purple and you couldn't tell about Judas either. Judas had hair the same color as the flowers. He was a traitor.

Roosevelt saw a rabbit, and he nearly stepped on

a snake with pretty black-and-orange patterns on its skin. He made a grab for the snake, but it slithered away and hid itself. Too bad. It would have been interesting to take it back to Quimby's Quarters. They could have put it up in the oak tree and tried to see if Sister's smile would charm it out the way Papa said.

Much too soon he came out of the woods and found himself beside the highway. That was no fun, so he turned around and ambled under the trees again, back along the stream and between the bean fields till he came to the thundery bridge and Quimby's Quarters.

There was the rather brown house, the porch and the curlycues, the oak tree, the pump, the junk pile, the washtub—but not one living soul to be seen or heard. Not a single sign of a human being. Not even Princess Anne. The washtub was empty.

The Whopper

Down Roosevelt's spine a chill crawled fast. It turned front and froze his stomach. For one single second that felt like a year, his feet stayed glued to the ground. Then they picked themselves up and streaked him into the house and up the stairs. He never once thought about breathing. He blew into the attic and braked to a stop.

Sunlight blurred in through the dormer windows and lighted up the middle. It left the corners dusky, but the place was empty. He could see that. Except for one lone horsefly buzzing against a windowpane, it was still as a graveyard. His heart thumped.

Roosevelt turned and flew down the stairs. He cleared the porch steps in one single bound. This time he raced around to the back of the house where he hadn't been before—and there they were: Mat-

thew and Sister and Princess Anne and the rest of the kids, and somebody else. A boy in a bright green jacket, sitting on a fallen tree.

Roosevelt's heart gave a little skip. He'd seen that boy before. He was nobody else in the world but that boy who had grabbed for the arithmetic paper. Manowar. And on his knee, looking happy as a baby chick and not missing Roosevelt one small bit, perched Princess Anne.

Roosevelt changed over quick from being scared to being glad. But he didn't stay glad. Nobody looked

at him. Nobody even saw him. Some of the boys and girls sat cross-legged on the ground and some sprawled over the fallen tree. All of them had their eyes and their ears fastened on Manowar. They were drinking in his talk as if it were cherry soda or good cold milk. The sight made Roosevelt cross, as cross as two sticks.

"Like I said," Manowar was telling them, "they had these geese. No man out there, not even the best old human cotton-chopper in the world, could get a job chopping cotton. You know why not?" He paused.

Trust old Matthew, the askingest boy in the whole country.

"Why not?" said Matthew.

"Why, because the geese chopped the cotton. All the cotton out there gets chopped by the geese, so the people can't get any jobs."

Out where? Where was Manowar talking about?

Chopping cotton meant cutting out the weeds. Roosevelt knew that. But how could geese chop cotton? How could a dumb goose tell a cotton seedling from a weed or a piece of grass? Now just how could a goose do that, Mister Manowar? A goose's not an intelligent animal, not like a dog or a horse, or a mule, even. You must be one awful whopper-teller, you Manowar, you. Roosevelt thought all this, but he didn't say it. He just stood there and listened like the others. Nobody paid the slightest attention to him. They didn't even know he was there.

Manowar went on. "Somebody found out, see, by accident kind of, he found this out—if you put a fence around your cotton field and if you turn a flock of geese inside the fence, the geese will grub out the weeds all right, but they won't touch the cotton. They won't touch it. You know why?"

The boys and girls shook their heads sideways. No, they didn't know. When Roosevelt found himself shaking his own head, he stopped in the middle of a shake. In case Manowar looked his way, he didn't want him to think he was interested.

"Here's why. Because the geese don't like the taste of a cotton plant. They'll eat all the grass and the weeds that's within their sight or smell, but they let the cotton stay. It's a sight to see. Those clumsy geese waddle in a line up one row till they hit the fence. Then they turn around and follow the head goose back down the next row, eating weeds all the way and passing up the cotton."

The sight tickled the audience. They giggled. All but Roosevelt, who scowled.

"When the farmer starts his geese out in the cotton, they're hardly any more than goslings—babies like Princess Anne here. But they get bigger. They grow up right along with the cotton, only the cotton grows up faster. So when the cotton gets to be taller than they are, the geese get scared. They can't see over the top, so they think they're in jail. They get panicky. They hiss and beat their wings and cut up a rumpus."

Sister squealed and ducked her head.

"That's all right, though, because by this time, the cotton's strong enough to choke out the weeds. So what does the farmer do with his geese?"

"Sells 'em," a boy called out.

"That's right. But first he feeds them pills and things to make them nice and fat for folks to eat. Then he sells them. To Chinese people. Not in China, though. In Chinatown. That's in San Francisco. Everybody who likes to eat geese goes to Chinatown,

and Chinatown restaurants buy every fat old goose
they can get a-hold of. So the farmers don't have to
pay any people to chop their cotton and they make
a fat profit on their fat geese. Big deal."

The boys and girls laughed and clapped their
hands.

San Francisco! But that's the city with the Golden
Gate and that's in California. Roosevelt knew that
much from school. Did this know-it-all Manowar
mean he'd seen all this goose stuff with his own two
eyes in California?

Roosevelt heard his own voice sing out, clear and
loud: "That's a whopper!"

The Showdown

Everybody looked at Roosevelt. Up to now they hadn't even noticed him.

"Hi," said Manowar. He grinned amiably, just as if he hadn't heard what Roosevelt said. "If it isn't the putting-into boy. How you doing, Kiddo?"

"You're a whopper-teller," said Roosevelt.

"What's that you say?"

What was the matter with Manowar? Couldn't he understand English?

"I said you're a whopper-teller. You told a whopper."

"Oh, you don't believe my story. Is that it?"

"That's it. How do you know what they do in California? That's a million miles away. It's three thousand miles. Have you been three thousand miles from here? Besides, you stole my baby sister out of the washtub. You hand her right back to me. Where she belongs."

The boys and girls watched, breathless. The new boy was two good sizes bigger than Princess Anne's brother. Would they fight?

Manowar lifted Princess Anne high up in the air and made as if he was going to throw her at Roosevelt. Quicker than you could see, Roosevelt jumped and grabbed for the baby. The jump knocked Manowar right back down on the ground with Roosevelt on top of him—but Manowar hung on to Princess Anne, and his two strong arms held her straight up in the air unhurt. She wasn't scared. She thought it was a game. She crowed.

Roosevelt pulled himself up on his knees and held out his arms to the baby. Whenever he did this, she always wanted to come. Not this time. She only turned her head away from him and stretched one hand down toward Manowar's face and crowed some more.

Roosevelt dropped his arms. He stood up, slow and dignified.

Manowar lay there flat on his back. He cuddled Princess Anne on his chest. He didn't say a word. But Roosevelt did.

"Do you want to get up and fight?"

With anybody his own size, Roosevelt was a middling good fighter. He was thin, but what he lacked in weight he made up in quick jabs. About Manowar, two sizes too large for him or maybe three, he didn't know. Never mind. He had to say it.

Manowar kept looking up at him. Finally the words came out, slow-like, as if he'd been asking himself a question and just found out the answer.

"No," he said. "I don't want to fight. First, see, I've got to get mad. And I'm not mad."

He chucked Princess Anne under the chin. "Baby," he said, "did you like my story? My true story? I can tell whoppers too. Someday I'll tell you a whopper. A real whopper."

"Now!"

"Tell it to us now!"

The cries came from all the boys and girls.

Manowar laughed. "Nope. Not now. I'm tired." He shut his eyes.

"The thing is," he went on, and now he opened his eyes and laughed out loud. "The thing is, I kind of like that putting-into kid. He's spunky." This time when he shut his eyes, they stayed shut and he pretended to go right off to sleep.

Roosevelt didn't say anything at all. He didn't have anything to say. Very slowly he turned his back on Manowar and Princess Anne and everybody. He walked around to the front of the house. He sat down on the porch steps with his elbows on his knees and he rested his chin on his two fists. He felt awful.

Probably he shouldn't have done what he did. Shouldn't have gone off and left Princess Anne in the washtub with nobody keeping her company. And now Princess Anne liked Manowar better than she liked him.

What did Mamma tell them? *You're scared somebody you like likes somebody else better than you.* That's jealous, she said. Was he jealous? Could just being jealous make you feel this bad? If he weren't nine years old and a boy, he'd cry.

He was glad about one thing, though. He wiped his nose on his sleeve. He was glad Manowar wasn't his older brother. He certainly was.

The Argument

When the beans were ready for picking, the whole Grady family went to the fields. Mamma and Papa argued about this and Papa won. Here's how the argument went:

"Beans are running good," said Papa. "Everybody up early tomorrow."

"Everybody?" said Mamma. "You and me, you mean."

"I mean everybody," said Papa.

"Not the children," said Mamma. "They're not going to work."

"What's wrong with work?" asked Papa. "Work never hurt anybody. The kids all picked strawberries in Louisiana, and Roosevelt's a crackerjack bean-picker."

"That doesn't make it right." Mamma didn't aim

to give up without trying, that was certainly plain.

"Oh, fiddle. It's a healthy thing for kids to work. They can't get hurt. Not when it's beans or berries or some easy thing like that. 'Tisn't like chopping cotton with a hoe or cutting asparagus with a knife."

Papa enjoyed arguments. Now he sounded half-way as if he was teasing Mamma. He and Matthew were just alike that way.

Papa went on: "Sister and Matthew better get in some practice on beans."

"Practice? Why should they practice?" Mamma's voice had an edge to it, sharp-like.

"Because they've got to learn sometime. Might as well begin now. It's a sure thing they'll have to pick when they grow up."

"Oh, they will, will they? That's what you think." Now Mamma was mad. She was mad clean through. Her eyes went from brown to black and turned shiny and they sparked. She really told Papa off.

"You just put this in your pipe and smoke it, Mister Henry Grady. My children are going to grow up to be something else besides stooping, crawling bean-pickers. They're going to get educated. Never you mind how. They're going to train for jobs where they stand up straight or sit down in back of a desk. They're going to be somebody." All of a sudden Mamma choked. A tear rolled right down her cheek. A real tear.

"Hey, there," said Papa, and he wasn't teasing any more. "I didn't know you felt all that bad about it."

For a minute he didn't say anything at all, and then he went on, "They're my kids, too, you know. Suppose they grew up to pick beans and the beans grew all in one place so they wouldn't have to go trucking around the country looking for them? Maybe even they'd be their own beans? Would you mind if they stooped over and crawled along after their very own beans?"

"Well," said Mamma, "well, I don't know. Maybe I wouldn't. But—oh, all right, you're so crazy to have them pick, let them pick. Only just so long as there isn't any school around for them to go to. When we come to a camp where there's a school, they're going to school. Understand? No more picking then."

"Okay," said Papa, "it's a deal. We get to a camp where there's a school, and we'll have no more picking. But tomorrow, everybody gets up early. Tomorrow everybody picks."

That's how Papa won the argument.

The Porch

The nicest part of the day at Quimby's Quarters turned out to be evenings after supper, and it was all on account of the porch.

Long after they left the Eastern Shore to go up the road with the season—weeks afterward and even years—Roosevelt would hear Mamma tell people about it. Neighbors, clerks in stores, strangers in a bus, any people at all she happened to be talking to, she'd tell them.

"Coming up from Florida," she'd say, "we worked three weeks on the Eastern Shore and our camp was a big old house with a wide front porch. Not a stoop, understand, a real porch. A piazza, it was. Nights after supper our whole family would sit out there on the piazza steps. We'd visit with ourselves, and sometimes other folks from the camp would join us. We'd sit and visit and sing and watch the dark drop down across the fields. It was lovely."

One night it was Cap Jackson who sat on the steps and visited with them.

Cap wasn't only the crew leader. He was a preacher, too, and he had a preachery voice, deep as purple velvet. Cap fell to talking about Digger Burton's crew. Camping on the other side of the woods across the highway, they were.

"His crew's not like ours," Cap said. "A noisy, rousty bunch of people he collects. He'll take on anybody, scrappers, dead beats, anybody at all just to get himself a crew."

Cap himself was particular. Roosevelt knew that. Everybody knew it. If somebody came along he didn't like the look of and if this person wanted to join his crew, Cap would say No. Like that. Just No, in that preachery voice of his, and they could see he meant it and no mistake.

"Digger gives them sweet talk about easy work and high pay and camps like motels with recreation rooms and television." Cap laughed. "Television! Oh, Digger's smooth all right. He'd do good himself on television, Digger would, getting folks to buy things they don't need. He gets those lazybones in his crew to thinking he's going to lead them all right into the Promised Land."

"It all depends, doesn't it," said Papa.

"What do you mean, it all depends?" asked Mamma.

"Depends on what you look to find in the Promised Land," said Papa.

Sister spoke up. "Won't the Promised Land be the same for everybody? Won't folks find just whatever's there when they get there?"

"Sister, I wonder," said Cap. "Your papa's got an

interesting idea there. Right interesting. Maybe there's a sermon in it." He turned to Mamma. "Addie, what do you look to find in the Promised Land?"

Roosevelt held his breath. He knew what Mamma hoped to find in the Promised Land or anyway, somewhere. A stay-put place where they'd all belong; that's what she wanted. But that was their secret, his and hers. Would she tell?

She didn't. What she said fitted in with the secret all right, but she didn't tell. Mamma was smart.

"My Promised Land will be a place where everybody has a chance," she said, "a place where everybody can be somebody."

"That's good, Addie. Very good." Cap nodded his head up and down. "The Lord would like that. He surely would. Henry, how about you? What kind of a Promised Land do you want?"

Roosevelt couldn't guess what Papa was going to say. When his answer came, it was a surprise, nice but more like a mother's answer than a father's. Kind of tender, it was.

"I look for the Promised Land to be a place where no little boy has to walk lame, not even if he's born with a bad foot. That's my Promised Land." Papa didn't say he had Matthew in his mind, but of course he did.

Roosevelt got to worrying about what he'd say when his turn came, but he needn't have bothered. Old Matthew jumped right in without waiting to be asked. He knew.

"My Promised Land's going to have a junk pile," he announced. "A big mountain of junk a hundred miles around. It'll reach up to the sky and it'll be busting full of treasures. Like this." And out of his pocket he pulled a little old battered harmonica and blew a squawk on it.

Everybody laughed. The spell was broken. No more sermon ideas for Cap that night. Cap stood up.

"There's one good thing about Digger's crew, though," he said. "It's that handy-boy of his. That Manowar. I'd like to have that boy around myself. He's a real good kid."

Roosevelt's stomach stiffened.

"Manowar's a good storyteller," said Sister. "He told us all about California."

"Yes, he did," said Matthew. "Do you know who chops the cotton in California? Manowar told us. It's the geese."

"Funny thing about those geese," said Cap. "They must be a sight to see."

Roosevelt's mouth felt dry. He started to speak and no words came. He swallowed and tried again. "Is that true, Cap? That about the geese?"

"Sure thing, it's true. My brother worked in California last year. He told me all about it. He found Manowar out there and brought him back east. Kind of on the loose, the boy was, after his granddaddy died."

"Where were the rest of his folks?" asked Mamma. "His mother and father and his uncles and his other kin?"

"There wasn't anybody but the old man, my brother said. Nobody was even sure the old man was the boy's real grandfather, but Manowar called him

Granddaddy, and it appeared the two of them had knocked around together all over the country. Came from Kentucky, way back, so folks said. The old man did, that is."

"Too bad the boy's tied up to Digger," Mamma declared. "That's not good."

"No, it's not," Cap agreed. "Well, good night, all." Cap turned and went in the house and they could hear him climbing the stairs. In a minute his voice floated down from the second-story window.

"Addie," he called, "Addie Grady. I just happened to think. Manowar's pretty well able to take care of himself. He was named for a race horse." Cap laughed and shut the window.

Up the Road

It was summer when the Gradys landed in a camp called Willowbrook.

Between Quimby's Quarters and Willowbrook was all a blur in Roosevelt's mind. The blur was made up of crops—asparagus, carrots, onions, broccoli, spinach, cucumbers, beans, you name it—all mixed up in Roosevelt's mind because as soon as they finished up carrots in one place and moved on north, there'd be carrots again just coming on. Beans were every place. If everybody in the United States ate beans three times a day for a year, they couldn't eat all the beans the Gradys picked that season. That's what Roosevelt decided.

They were in onions when Roosevelt took sick. First it was just sniffles. They mostly all had sniffles a lot of the time, but this time Roosevelt couldn't eat anything at all and he could hardly hold his head up.

Cap Jackson had to drive his truck to town to get his brakes fixed, so he carried Mamma and Roosevelt along with him and he hunted up a doctor for them. Matthew went too, just for the ride.

Roosevelt had never been to a doctor before. You might suppose he was too sick to notice much, but afterward he could remember a lot about that visit. The doctor was pink-cheeked and yellow-haired and young, and he wore a stiff white coat that smelled clean. He thumped Roosevelt and made him hold a glass pencil in his mouth. His name was Doctor Bates. He took out the glass pencil and looked at it.

"The boy's got a bug. That's all," said Doctor Bates. "Just a flu bug flew in and bit him. We'll fix him up. You keep him in bed a day or two and give him plenty of orange juice and milk. Fresh milk. Better keep him in a room by himself. Be sure to scald the glass he drinks out of, and his dishes and silver, too. Every time he uses them. And these pills—a pink one every hour and two white ones every three hours till they're gone."

Roosevelt wondered how Mamma would know when it was one hour and three hours. They didn't have any clock and nobody in the family had a watch. Probably if you just guessed about it, you'd hit it close enough.

Doctor Bates gave him a balloon and he gave one to Matthew, too. His was red and Matthew's was green. Then he said to Matthew, "Let me see that foot."

Matthew's feet were bare. He held up his bad foot and Doctor Bates felt of it, all around.

"Why didn't you have something done about this foot three years ago?" he said to Mamma, rather cross-like. "I might be able to help it some even now, if you'll let me keep him in the hospital three months. I don't know, but I can try."

So far Mamma hadn't said much. Not anything, really. Just nodded Yes to everything Doctor Bates said. But now she looked fixing to make a speech. And she did.

"Doctor Bates," she said, "I think I'd best tell you something. We follow the crops for a living. Right now we're living in one room, all six of us. We got no clock to measure taking medicine by. We got no icebox. What we eat with, it isn't silver, it's tin, but we keep it clean. We fetch our water from a community spigot and I heat it on an oil stove.

"About Matthew's foot, his papa and I, we never knew it might be fixed. Even if we had the money to pay to leave him in the hospital, the Lord alone knows where we'll be in three months time, and He may be in some doubt Himself. Folks got to do what they can with what they got and that's what we do.

We make out. And thank you kindly, Doctor Bates. How much do I owe you for these pills?"

When Mamma stopped talking, Doctor Bates looked younger even than he had before. He looked like a little boy the teacher had scolded. He stared out the window, and then:

"Mrs. Grady," he said, "a lot of people have been in my office from that farm-labor camp where you're staying, but none of them ever explained to me what it's like. I figure what you've told me is worth as much to me as those pills are worth to you. So we're even."
Then he shook hands with Roosevelt and with Matthew.

"You're sure?" said Mamma. "I don't want to be beholden."

"I'm sure," said Doctor Bates. "If anybody is beholden, it's not you." He walked to the door with them. "Good-by, Mrs. Grady," he said, and he shook hands with Mamma.

The pills worked fine, and if it hadn't been for the trip to the doctor, Roosevelt wouldn't have even remembered that he'd been sick.

On the way north they lost track of Digger Burton's crew. Cap Jackson's truck left Quimby's Quarters the same day Digger's outfit took off, but Digger traveled faster. He carried his people in a yellow bus, not new, but it made good time. Cap's truck kept breaking down like always, and you can't make time when you have to wait over a day to get the carburetor soldered. So all those weeks they never did see Manowar. But on the way to Willowbrook there was one camp where they stopped and they knew he'd been there. How did they know? That's easy. The boys and girls in that camp were all playing a

game called Geese in the Cotton. It was a game made up right out of Manowar's California story.

One day as they were going north, Cap Jackson let Roosevelt and Matthew and Sister ride alongside of him right up in the front of the truck. They begged him to tell them about Willowbrook.

"Willowbrook? It's a whale of a camp," he told them. "Room for half a dozen crews like ours. Maybe more. Must be twenty cabins all hitched together in a single row. And they have three rows like that. Fill up three sides of a square, they do. A great big hollow square, one row of cabins to each side. Right in the middle of the square there's a shack with cookstoves in it for folks that don't bring along their own stoves the way your mamma does. The cookshack has a juke box in it, too, and a loud-speaker so I can call my folks to come when it's time to cash in their bean tickets."

Roosevelt knew what that meant. So did Sister and Matthew. When you've picked your hamperful of beans, you drag it off to be weighed and then you get a ticket, and later on Papa trades in the ticket for money. Fifty cents, seventy-five cents, something like that, depending on how big the hamper is and what they are paying that day. Florida hampers weigh thirty-two pounds, sometimes, when they're full.

"How'll I know which cabin's ours?" asked Matthew. "If they're hitched together and they all look alike, how'll I know when I'm home?"

"You'll get to know. Each cabin has its own door with a number on it to tell you which one your family belongs in. Has its own window, too."

"A square has four sides. You told us about three of them. What's on the fourth side of the square?" Roosevelt wanted to know. "The empty side?"

"Guess," Cap ordered.

"Willow-brook. A brook. I guess a brook. And fish in it." That was Matthew.

"Wrong," said Cap.

"I guess a willow tree," said Sister. "Nice and droopy with lots of shade to play in."

"Wrong."

"A schoolhouse?" asked Roosevelt. He was quite sure this was not the right answer. He was only hoping.

"All wrong," said Cap. "No brook, and I don't recall seeing a willow tree anywhere around. The name of that camp's a fake. No school, either. There's a big brick school building five miles down the road for the resident children, but there isn't any school at Willowbrook."

"Then what does fill up the empty side of the hollow square?" asked Matthew. "Tell us, Cap. We give up."

"Beans," said Cap. "A bean field, right on the doorstep."

When they finally came to Willowbrook, sure enough there was the hollow square with the cook-shack in the middle and on the square's empty side, the bean field. No brook. No willow tree. No school-house. And no sign of Digger Burton's crew.

Willowbrook Camp

The way it worked at Willowbrook, your papa stood in line at the cookshack door and waited his turn for a man called Bucky to say which cabin his family could have. Bucky was the camp manager. His entire name was Bucky Bean, and he ran things at Willowbrook.

"Bucky Bean?" With his index finger, Matthew scoured out his right ear and then his left, making believe he hadn't heard right. "Is his name really and truly Bean? Mr. Bucky Bean?"

"Must be," Mamma answered. "That's what your papa said, and I don't know why he'd make it up."

"Ho—ho—ho," said Matthew. "Mr. Bean's in charge of beans." He thumped on his chest with his fists and limped around in a circle, chanting:

> Mister Bean
> What I mean
> Pick 'em clean
> Or ol' man Bean
> He'll get himself
> A bean machine!

"Matthew!" Mamma spoke sharp. "Where'd you hear that?"

"No place. It just popped out of my mouth. Don't you like it? I do. Do you want some more? Bean—seen—green—queen—screen—"

Just then Papa came back from standing in line.

"Number Seven," he announced. "That's where we belong. See who can find it first."

On each cabin door there was painted in black a huge sprawly number. It should have been easy to find Cabin Number Seven, but it wasn't. There was something queer about those numbers.

Sister was the first to spot Number Seven and while Roosevelt was still puzzling in his head, she figured out what was the matter. Times were when Sister promised to grow up as smart as Mamma, and this was one of those times.

"There's ours," she cried and she darted over to a door and pointed.

"That's no seven," said Roosevelt. He was tired and

cross, and he guessed he knew what a seven ought to look like.

"Maybe it's not a seven," said Sister, "but the man who painted it thought it was. Look." And pointing, she counted out the cabins backwards to the beginning of the row: "Seven, Six, Five, Four, Three, Two, One. This one's Number Seven, all right."

The figures looked like this:

$$\text{Γ∂ᘔ4∈ՐΙ}$$

"That old Camp Manager Bucky Bean must have let a first grader do his painting for him," said Roosevelt, crosser than ever because he hadn't located Number Seven ahead of Sister.

"Maybe," said Sister, "but whoever did it, he looks at things through a looking glass. Backwards!" She giggled, and so did everybody else, even Roosevelt. Once you knew what was the matter, the figures did look comical.

Roosevelt lugged his mother's metal suitcase into Cabin Number Seven and set it in the middle of the floor. Then he ran back outdoors to have a look around the camp. He walked along, counting cabins. Starting from the bean field, the three sides of the hollow square had twenty cabins to a side. Just what Cap said. Times three, that made sixty families. Suppose every family was like the Gradys and had six people to it; there could be six times sixty people living in that camp. Six times sixty: 360 folks. Could mean as many as seven or eight crews, nine or ten, even. Not that many now, because the whole far side of the square stood padlocked and empty.

But just suppose. Suppose you had ten crew leaders and each one picked out crews as different from each other as Cap Jackson and Digger Burton did. And suppose half the crew leaders didn't like the other half any better than Cap liked Digger. There'd sure enough be plenty of chance for quarrelings.

Cabin Number Eight had a fat lady living in it named Mrs. Clay. She was big enough to fill up the cabin with no help from anybody else, but besides herself there were her husband James, skinny and sour-looking, and a large collection of children, all girls.

The Gradys hadn't been one hour at Willowbrook before they found themselves acquainted with Pearly Ann Clay because Pearly Ann was seven years old and so was Sister and right away they started being girl friends. But nobody in the Grady family had the rest of the Clays sorted out until Matthew met Mrs. Clay.

It was the next day. Mrs. Clay had just finished her wash and was hanging out her clothes on a line stretched across from her cabin to the cookshack roof. Her clothespins were in a bucket on the ground, so

she would put half a dozen of the pins in her mouth at once and pull them out one at a time as she needed them. She had a wide mouth to suit the rest of her. It accommodated six clothespins without stretching.

Mrs. Clay hadn't noticed Matthew at all, and when he said to her, "Mrs. Clay, how many children have you got?" she was so startled she blew the clothespins right out of her mouth and they flew every which way. Matthew limped around picking them up and when he brought them back, he said:

"How about if I hand these to you one at a time out of the bucket? That way we can have a satis-fac-tory conversation."

Mrs. Clay gave Matthew a rather peculiar look, but:

"Let's try," she said. Matthew handed her a clothespin. "Now then. What did you ask me?"

"How many children have you got?"

"Well, let me see," said Mrs. Clay. "We'll start at the top. Two clothespins this time, please. There." She set the two pins firmly into a pair of blue jeans. "That's Marlene and Cherry. Twins."

Matthew handed her another pin.

"This is Lulubelle. Now two more, please. These are Sue Ellen and Tillie: twins again." Now it was diapers she was hanging up. She reached down her hand to Matthew for another pin. "And one for little Baby Bethalene. Six girls, and they're all mine.

"Now one for Wanda. She's the child of Clay's brother and she's the size of my Marlene and Cherry. Wanda scraps with her own folks so she mostly travels with us. That's seven."

"And Pearly Ann," said Matthew, handing up another clothespin.

"And Pearly Ann," said Mrs. Clay. "She makes eight. Eight girls. That's how many children I've got."

"Where'd Pearly Ann come from?" persisted Matthew.

"Pearly Ann?" Mrs. Clay hung up the last dress in her basket. Thin blue-and-white stripes it had, and she kind of smoothed it out with her hands as she talked. "When Pearly Ann was a mite of a baby, no longer than a shoe box, her mamma died. Down in South Carolina, in the strawberries, it was. Her papa, he was half crazy, he felt so bad to lose his wife, and he said to me, 'What am I going to do with Pearly Ann?' So I said, 'You give Pearly Ann to me and don't you fret. I'll look after her just as easy, right along with mine. One extra isn't going to be a speck more bother than what I've got already.' And that's the way it's been. Seven years now and Pearly Ann fits in with us so good, I declare I mostly disremember she didn't start out being my baby at all."

When Matthew felt like working his memory, there was nothing he couldn't recall. That night the Gradys heard every word of his talk with Mrs. Clay, exactly the way it happened.

The thought of those clothespins tickled Papa so hard he choked. He had to wipe his eyes before he could speak one word.

"There's one thing about you, Matthew," he said.

"What's one thing about me?" asked Matthew.

Papa picked him up and set him on his knee. Very gently he rubbed his feet, the good one and the bad one. Then he put a finger under Matthew's chin and tipped up his face.

"There's nothing wrong with your head," Papa told him. "Or your funny bone."

Mamma was struck to know about all those Clay children.

"Think of that," said Mamma. "Six girls of her own and two more that don't rightly belong to her, but she keeps them in the family just as if they did. I could be wrong, but that man of hers looks to me to be no help at all. And that poor South Carolina strawberry-picker who lost his wife, her telling him one more child wouldn't be a speck of bother. What's more, I do believe she meant it. I declare, I'm going to talk to that woman. Find out how she does it. I marvel at her."

"You have anything in mind?" asked Papa, in his teasing voice. Before Mamma could answer he went to speaking serious. "Addie Grady, I do say this and I want you to hearken to it. You have no call to marvel at any other woman. How ever many extra children she adds on to her family, she can't beat you. You're the best."

"Henry Grady," said Mamma, tossing her head. "How you talk." But she did look pleased.

Beans were running good, and soon sweet corn began to come along. One day Papa brought home a big basket of runty ears, good to eat but so small the packing house wouldn't take them, so Bucky Bean told Papa he could carry them home.

"This is a sight more corn than we can eat," said Mamma. She took a good bit over half of the ears and gave them to Mrs. Clay. The two of them sat in their doorways and husked the corn. Roosevelt helped. He liked to pull off the long green jackets and then go after every bit of silk and grub it out.

Mrs. Clay told Mamma: "Fresh corn. This is a treat. We've had a rough season, me and Clay and the girls." She didn't call her husband James, or James Clay, or Mr. Clay; just Clay. "Willowbrook is the first place our crew has been in five weeks where there's anything like regular work."

"Is that a fact!" said Mamma. "And all those girls to feed."

"Clay eats a-plenty, too. He may look small, but it takes a powerful quantity of victuals to keep his strength up. We didn't starve, though. Over in Lakeland County when the drouth burned up the beans, they fixed it for us to get food from the government. Surplus, they called it. Stuff nobody will buy and they save it for when folks get hungry. Dried milk and flour and rice and like that. Cheese, too. You could do a right tasty dish from it. Oh, yes, and peanut butter. That kept it from being tiresome. It's a caution what use you can make out of peanut butter."

"Did the dry spell kill all the beans in Lakeland County?" Mamma asked.

"Not all, no, but there was another thing. Machines."

"Machines," said Mamma. "I keep hearing and hearing, but I never saw one yet. Not to pick beans with, I didn't. Tell me."

"Oh, they have 'em all right. One place where we've gone for years—Mr. Simmons—we went there and he'd beat the drouth by irrigating so his beans were good, but over the winter he'd bought himself a bean-picking machine. He let us stay and do a field once over by hand, but then he turned in the machine and stripped it clean. That machine really finished up the crop. Once over and that's it."

"They must cost a pile of money, those machines."

"That's what Bucky Bean told Clay. 'We don't go for the machines,' he told him. Besides the cost,

Bucky's boss figures to get more beans to the acre when people do the picking. He can plant the rows closer together when he uses people, and he can have three, four, even five pickings to a field. And the machine tears the beans, too. Hand-picked beans bring in a good bit better price on the market."

"Still, the time will come," said Mamma.

"Sure the time will come." Mrs. Clay nodded her head. "But meanwhile I don't aim to worry. Not yet, I don't."

"What don't you aim to worry about, Mrs. Clay?" said Papa, who had sauntered up. He took the last ear of corn away from Mamma and began to husk it.

"Mechanical bean-pickers," Mrs. Clay answered. "That's what I don't figure to let trouble my sleep. Life is short enough if you take what comes without trying to foretell future events."

"But what's it going to do to us?" said Mamma. "When they get machines to harvest everything? Machines for carrots and onions and cucumbers and spinach and all like that?"

"And strawberries," said Roosevelt.

Mamma went on. "There won't be any jobs at all, not for folks like us, there won't. Folks who live on the season."

Papa finished husking his ear and tossed it into the basket.

"Strawberries," he said. "I should live to see the

day they get a machine to pick strawberries. Addie, it looks as if Mrs. Clay and I are great believers in Providence. Plug along and rest easy and trust in Providence to come up with something when the time is right."

"Providence is well and good," said Mamma, snappy-like, "but sometimes it can use help from folks."

"Maybe it's that folks don't always see so plain what Providence throws their way," said Papa. "Anyway, Providence fixed it for us to have a nice mess of corn for dinner tonight, didn't it? When do we eat?"

Sunday Night

They had been at Willowbrook two weeks when two special things happened, both on the same Sunday night.

The first one happened right after supper. Over the loud-speaker a message came that didn't have anything at all to do with cashing in bean tickets. The loud-speaker crackled and rumbled and then the words came clear.

"All parents," blared the voice, and it wasn't Cap Jackson speaking or any other crew leader. It was Camp Manager Bucky Bean. "All parents come to the cookshack. Right away. Mothers and fathers, you got any kids, you come to the cookshack. Now."

What could this mean? Had some boy or girl done something bad? Roosevelt couldn't stand it not to know. He tagged along behind his mother and father.

88

There were more parents milling around the cook-shack door than could possibly get inside. Roosevelt stood on the edge of the crowd, hiding behind Mrs. Clay, and listened. It was not bad news. It was good. Too good to be true, almost. He couldn't believe his ears.

School, the man said. It wasn't Bucky Bean who told them. It was another man, a stranger, who said there was going to be a school for all the children from the farm-labor camps anywhere around. That's what he said.

The man was tall and thin and he had on a dark blue dress-up suit—coat and necktie and all—and he stood right there in the cookshack door and told them. It was a special school, he said, a school only for their children. Any boy or girl, five years or older could go. Nobody else. Not resident children. Starting in the morning and every day for three weeks, Mondays straight through Fridays, a bus would come by to pick up the children. Eight o'clock.

Not all the parents liked this so very much. They mumbled some among themselves, and a few talked right up.

"What good will school do my girls?" asked Mrs. Clay. "My Lulubelle went to school three different places last winter and now she's a slower bean-picker than she was before she went." The people laughed.

"No call for my kids to go to school," said one

father. "Not in the summer. Their brains need a rest."

"How do you figure my boy's going to help me earn a living and him in school all day?" asked another.

The dressed-up man seemed to understand how each of them felt, but he kept right on.

"Nobody's going to make you send your children to school, not if there's a good reason for them not to go," he explained. "But so far I haven't heard anybody give a good reason. If your children are under twelve years old, the law in this state says they mustn't work in the fields. So they might as well be in school. Now about those brains needing a rest. A brain is a lot like a machine. When it doesn't get used, it gets rusty. It won't work. That's the way it is with a person's brain. It needs exercise. If a person doesn't use his brain, it stops working."

One mother fretted about clothes. "Oscar can't go. He left his school clothes down in Florida."

"That won't matter," the dressed-up man assured her. "Work clothes or play clothes, either one will do fine."

Roosevelt didn't wait to hear another word. The Gradys could go to the school, that he knew. His father had promised his mother they could, that day he won the argument. Papa was not one to break a promise. Roosevelt raced back to their cabin to tell Sister and Matthew.

The second special thing happened in the middle of the night.

Roosevelt and Matthew were sleeping right underneath the window on a prickly straw-stuffed mattress tick. The tick was old and worn thin in spots, so the straw poked out and pricked you in unexpected places. Old Matthew couldn't care less. Not seven stubborn mattress straws scratching at his skin in seven different places could keep him awake, and once he was asleep, a hundred hound dogs baying at the moon wouldn't budge him.

This particular night was warm and sticky, too hot for covers. Matthew had hit the middle of the mattress stomach-down with his arms up over his head. The minute he landed he went out like a light. No use trying to move him over to one side or the other. Long ago Roosevelt had given that up; it was like pushing at the Blue Ridge Mountains. He eyed the spaces left on either side of Matthew, finally crawled across him to the window space, and rolled and squirmed until he had the straw tame enough for him to rest comfortably.

But he couldn't go to sleep. He was too excited about school. Moonlight slanted in through the window and seemed to filter through his lashes straight into his tight-shut eyes. Inside his head, school thoughts and wonderings kept churning round and round and bumping each other. He was so stirred up, he wouldn't get to sleep the whole night through; that's what he expected. Yet after a while he must have dropped off. If he hadn't, how could something wake him up? And it did.

A roar, first, of a motor chugging by the Grady window and coming to a dead stop just beyond. A whoopy yell, then shrieks and laughs and high-pitched talk, all mixed up together and shrill. Must be another crew moved in. A noisy one, for sure. As noisy as Digger Burton's.

Digger Burton!

Roosevelt came clean awake and opened his eyes wide to the moonlit dark. Out of the conglomeration of sounds, voices began to separate themselves. One was Digger Burton's, all right. A boy's voice halfway between a scream and a sob, cried "Stop! Stop!" And then Cap Jackson's boom, not purple velvet now but scarlet red and mad.

"Digger! Drop that knife! Drop it, I say! Digger! Let go of that boy!"

Thumping feet, a scuffle, and Digger Burton's voice, oily, mocking.

"Why, Cap, you know old Digger. You know he wouldn't go for to hurt anybody. Leastways a little boy. All Digger's doing is teasing, only having a spot of fun and showing that little old Manowar how to take a joke. No harm in that, now, is there?"

Roosevelt scrambled to his knees and peered out the window. The moon lit up Digger's long yellow bus and outlined dark knots of people, not yelling now but still as statues. It was like watching a giant hold his breath.

There in an open space stood Cap. His back was straight as a telegraph pole and his shadow looked bigger than a house. Papa always said Cap was strong as an ox and too bad he had to be a preacher, he'd have made a great prize fighter. Now Cap had that puffy fat Digger by the wrists and forced halfway to his knees. All at once the fingers in Digger's right hand must have gone limp, for something silver left it and flashed to the ground. The knife, that could be. Cap let go of Digger's wrists, and Digger sat flat down in the dirt, hard.

Cap dusted off his hands. He stooped down and picked up the knife, snapped it shut, and put it in his pocket.

"Manowar?" he called. "Manowar, where are you? Are you all right?"

Out of the shadows a shaky voice answered. "Hi, Cap. I'm all right." Manowar's figure moved into the moonlight. "Here I am. Thanks." Roosevelt had always thought of Manowar as a big boy, but standing there beside Cap he did look small. Certainly not two sizes bigger than Roosevelt. Cap laid his arm around Manowar's shoulders.

Digger was still sitting on the ground, rubbing his wrists. Cap looked down at him.

"Digger Burton," he said, "the next time you want

to have a little fun, pick on somebody your own size. You're here at Willowbrook now, and so am I. You and your crew and me and mine, we have to live together for a piece and we don't want any trouble.

But sure as you take out your meanness on that boy Manowar or anybody else that's not full grown, trouble is what you'll be looking for and trouble is what you'll find. Hear me?"

Digger grunted, but Cap didn't wait to listen.

"Manowar," he said, "you're sleeping in our cabin tonight." And just as if Manowar were no bigger than Princess Anne, Cap picked him up and held him in his arms like a baby. Then more like a soldier than a preacher he swiveled on his heel and off he went into the dark. In a minute his cabin door slammed.

The people shifted their feet, murmured, and began moving away toward the row of empty cabins on the far side of the square. After a minute Digger rolled over on his knees. He stood up, stamped his feet, and stepped off wobbly-like, sort of trying out his legs. They appeared to work and he moved along after his crew.

Roosevelt stayed on at the window, his chin resting on the sill. The sounds dwindled down to nothing. Willowbrook Camp grew still as a graveyard.

So. Manowar was here. Right in time for school, too, if he wanted to go. If Digger Burton would let him go. Probably Digger wouldn't dare not let him go, not with Cap around.

Roosevelt's eyelids fluttered shut. He slumped down on the mattress and fell into an uneasy dream. In the bean field they were, all Cap Jackson's crew and Digger Burton's crew, Manowar and everybody, all picking. The dressed-up man who'd stood in the cookshack door was there, too. He sat on a bottom-side-up bean hamper with wheels underneath it and he rolled along up and down the bean rows, smiling and holding up a piece of a broken blackboard, with crooked looking-glass letters printed on it, reading:

ƔAᗡoT ⅃o°HↄƧ

And all the time the dressed-up man kept sing-songing: "Brains get rusty . . . come and study . . . study putting into . . . putting into . . . putting into . . ."

And then it was morning.

Mrs. Dinwiddie

There were four separate classes in the Willowbrook school and the one you went into depended on how old you were. Matthew went with the five and six year olds, Sister with the sevens and eights, and Roosevelt with the nines, tens, elevens. Manowar showed up in this class, too. And then there was one for the big boys and girls, twelve and up, only this one didn't have many pupils in it except on rainy days.

Roosevelt's class wasn't ready yet for putting into, but on the blackboard, Mrs. Dinwiddie showed him privately how to fix up the left-over number.

"You make a little shelf," she explained, "like this: ———— . You put something underneath it to hold it up. Like this: $\dfrac{}{3}$. Then on top you set the left-over number. Like this: $\dfrac{2}{3}$.

"There. See? The left-over number can rest safe and comfortable while you're waiting to need it. How's that?"

"Good," said Roosevelt. "It's a good idea. I wonder why I didn't think of doing that myself."

Mrs. Dinwiddie had no stick. She did not look teachery. Too young, for one thing. Too small, for another. She had cornsilk hair and if she hadn't worn shoes with spiky heels, she wouldn't have been much taller than Roosevelt. Her sweater and her skirt were both sky blue and she kept pushing her sweater sleeves up above her elbows. When she walked around the room, her high heels went *click-click-click* on the floor so you knew where she was whether you were looking that way or not.

Lulubelle Clay, the slow bean-picker, saw she was different, too.

"Mrs. Dinwiddie," asked Lulubelle, "are you a real teacher?"

"Yes, Lulubelle, I am," Mrs. Dinwiddie answered. "At least I'm a teacher. Are you real, Lulubelle? If you're real, then I'm real, too." She held out her arm. "Here. Pinch." The class held its breath. Lulubelle pinched. "How about it? Am I real?"

"Yes," said Lulubelle. "You're real."

"Tell me, Lulubelle, why did you think maybe I wasn't real?"

"I don't know," said Lulubelle, "only most generally the teacher has a stick and she whips me to make me read." Lulubelle grinned. "I still can't read."

"We'll fix that," said Mrs. Dinwiddie. "Reading is nothing else but understanding talk through your eyes instead of through your ears. It's not so hard."

Mrs. Dinwiddie was great on stories. How you tell if a story is good, she said, is if people keep quiet and listen while you tell it to them. If the story is good enough, you don't have to tell them to keep still. They won't remember to wiggle; they'll be too interested. A story doesn't have to be true. It may be true or it may not be true—it's nice to know which—but what's important is, does the audience like it. Audience. They're the people you want to get to listen to your story. Or to read it, once you get it written down. Writing is nothing else but talk written down.

Everyone in the class had a chance to tell a story. Roosevelt called his, "My Brother Matthew." He made it true because he wasn't so good at inventing stories. He told about old Matthew and his jokes and how he bumped his head a-purpose on the attic roof and how he was always finding something interesting everywhere he went and especially about him crawling around the junk pile at Quimby's Quarters and coming up with a beat-up old harmonica that squawked. The boys and girls liked this story quite well. Anyway they listened without a wiggle, and at the end, they laughed and clapped their hands.

When Manowar's turn came, he stood up and announced: "Mine's a whopper."

His story took off something like Jack and the Beanstalk. He told about a boy named Joshway, who found an old tomato can and filled it with dirt and planted a sunflower seed in it. At least it looked to Joshway like a sunflower seed, but later on, he was not so sure. Joshway watered the dirt every day and after a while the seed sprouted and then it grew very fast and very big. Some days it grew as much as a foot before lunch.

Wherever Joshway went, from one ripe crop to another, he toted his plant along, from carrots to onions to cauliflower and so on. Finally the plant got as tall as a telephone pole, and it grew such fine spready branches that Joshway built a platform high up on a couple of the branches and fixed himself a small house among the shiny green leaves.

One day a pair of catbirds flew in and asked him if he minded if they built themselves a nest in his tree. On the opposite side from his own house, of course, they explained. Joshway decided he'd let them do it, thinking if they weren't too close, he might enjoy their company.

Another day he woke up in the morning and found a possum hanging from a branch by its tail. The possum didn't ask permission. He stayed on without a by-your-leave and he was no bother to Joshway because he appeared not to do anything ever except sleep.

All this time the tree was growing at the bottom too. Tough snaky roots broke through the tomato can and split it all to pieces and they crept down into the ground. These roots did their growing at night mostly. Every morning Joshway would pull them out of the ground, and every night the roots would go back down in, each time a little deeper. Came a

morning when Joshway found he couldn't pull them
out. They were stuck fast. It was time to move on to
another crop, but he couldn't leave the tree behind
and his house and all. So there was nothing for it
but he had to stay and live there in his tree house.
He got rather hungry, not having any work, but by
and by folks took to coming along and wanting to pay
rent for branches to build houses on for themselves.
Pretty soon Joshway had every pocket full of paper
money and he had enough people living in his tree to
make two sides for a softball game.

Here Manowar stopped talking and walked over
to the drinking fountain and took a good long gulp.

"Is that the end?" asked Lulubelle.

"No," said Manowar, coming back from the
fountain. "A bulldozer came rolling along and a cat
was driving it. A big fierce cat he was, black-and-
yellow stripes and extra-long whiskers. The cat said,
'I'll give you five minutes to move out, and then I'm
going to run right over your tree, houses and all.'

"Joshway had to think fast. He thought for three
minutes. Then he whispered something to the catbirds and that took another minute. The birds
bobbed their heads and chirped and fluttered their
wings. Then he whispered something to the possum,
who kept his eyes shut and gave no more sign of life
than he ever had.

"Right then the cat decided the five minutes were

up. He started the bulldozer bearing down on the tree.

" 'Go,' Joshway shouted, and the catbirds flew straight at the bulldozer, and the cat jumped up in the air to catch them and their feathers flew. The possum leaped down from his branch and coiled his tail around the steering wheel. The bulldozer slipped sideways and scraped past the tree, taking only a small chip out of its trunk. Faster and faster went the bulldozer, the possum still hanging on and the cat racing after it until they were all clean out of sight.

"Joshway breathed long and deep.

" 'The possum doesn't worry me,' he said. 'He can look after himself. It's too bad about the catbirds, though. I'll miss having them around.' "

"And right then he heard, 'Meow, meow,' and he looked up and there were the catbirds sitting on their nest with their breasts all swelled up looking as though they'd swallowed the bulldozer.

" 'Hi,' said Joshway. 'Glad you made it back. Great job you did. Much obliged.' He climbed up into his tree house and sat down and began to eat his lunch. 'I guess I was wrong,' he said to himself.

" 'Wrong about what?' the catbirds asked, both at once, expecting more praise.

" 'Wrong about that seed I planted in the tomato can,' said Joshway. 'I guess it couldn't have been a sunflower seed, after all.' "

That afternoon Roosevelt was the last one to get on the school bus. He had to take the only seat left. It was next to Manowar.

"Where you been?" asked Manowar. "I been saving this seat for you."

"Why?" asked Roosevelt, not looking at him.

"Why not?" asked Manowar.

"Because I was wrong."

"Wrong about what?"

"Wrong about those geese. In California. That *was* a true story. Cap Jackson told me."

"Oh, that," said Manowar.

"I'm sorry," said Roosevelt.

"Forget it. Besides," and Manowar laughed— "this shows I was right about the other thing, too."

"Right about what other thing?" asked Roosevelt.

"Right about you," said Manowar. "You got spunk."

After School

The first two weeks at Willowbrook had crept along so drab and poky, every minute seemed to last an hour. But when school began, time took off *whoosh!* like a rocket and shot into the air. Mrs. Dinwiddie kept things a-stir at school every single second, and afternoons when school let out, there was always something interesting to do with Manowar around.

Cap Jackson must have scared Digger Burton for fair. Digger let Manowar go to school every day and he thought up hardly any chores for him to do.

Some days after school the big boys set a softball game going, and they let Roosevelt and Manowar field for them.

One time the two boys dropped in to say hello to Cap Jackson and found him busy with his book-keeping, so they helped him add up figures. Mrs. Jackson gave them cookies and lemonade.

Another day Manowar took Roosevelt to see his cabin over on the far side of the hollow square. It had four double-decker beds in it, one against each wall. Making a sort of curtain to divide the cabin cater-corner were some men's clothes hanging from a rope. Roosevelt recognized the green corduroy jacket.

" 'Tisn't all exactly mine," Manowar explained. "I hole in with seven other fellows in Digger's crew. See, here's where I sleep," and he pointed to the top bunk on the back wall.

"Neat," said Roosevelt. "A bed all to yourself. The only time I ever had a bed all mine was the hammock in that attic at Quimby's Quarters. I could kick and swing and nobody cared. It was great." He looked around. "Where do you cook?"

"We don't have to bother with food," said Manowar. "The lady in the next cabin cooks for us and for Digger, too. It works okay."

A red-and-white bundle of something tied with a string swung from the iron pipe running across the foot of Manowar's bunk.

"What's that?" asked Roosevelt.

"What?" said Manowar. "Oh, that. That's mine. Just a few things I carry around with me. Want to see them?"

The boys scrambled up on the top bunk. Manowar

untied the red-and-white bandana and spread out the contents.

"Five treasures," he said, "all mine. This one's a piece of petrified wood from Arizona. See those pretty colors? You can hardly think it used to be part of a tree, but it did."

"Where'd you get the silver star?" asked Roosevelt.

"It's silvery but 'tisn't silver. It's tin. It was on top of a Christmas tree. One time in a camp in Arkansas they had a Christmas party with a tree, ice cream and games and races and all like that. At the end they took the star off the tree and made it to be a prize for the fifty-yard dash. I won. But this is really silver." He took up a heavy necklace and hung it around his neck.

"An Indian man gave me this. A Navaho. New Mexico, that was, in the carrots. Danny Yazzie. He hammered out the silver to make these little flowers. Squash blossoms, they are. They look to be alike, but see? Every one is a tiny bit different from every other one. Danny wore this all the time."

Roosevelt was impressed. "An Indian! Weren't you scared of him?"

"Shucks, no. Danny was a great guy. Been in the army and couldn't wait to get back and herd sheep. Every once in a while he'd take off with his folks and go on the carrots or the onions, but what he really liked were sheep. He took a shine to me. Wanted me to go back to the reservation with him and help with his sheep. Said I'd make a good Indian because I knew when to keep my mouth shut. When I went to say good-by he didn't say a word. Just took this necklace off his own neck and hung it around mine."

He lifted the necklace over his head and laid it gently down on the bandana.

"Who made this horse?" Roosevelt stroked a little wooden figure. "How'd he get the wood so soft? It feels like silk. Even its curly mane."

"Granddaddy. He carved it out of applewood just for me, and he rubbed it down with sandpaper and turpentine and linseed oil. Said it was my mascot."

"Mascot. What's that?"

"It's supposed to bring good luck. Granddaddy gave me this book too. He taught me to read with it. Hard going in spots, but there's some great stories in it. Here, I'll show you the best." He flipped through the pages. "Here it is. *The Luck of Roaring Camp.* Granddaddy said the baby in this story put him in mind of me. No reason, though, because that kid stood on his head for five minutes running, and I could never last more than two. Besides, this story ends up sad."

Manowar slammed the book shut. "Come on. Let's go." He tied up the five treasures in the kerchief and hung the bundle back on the iron pipe. "Let's go see Princess Anne."

"Okay. I'll race you as far as the cookshack." Roosevelt bounded off the top bunk and made for the door.

"Hey! Wait a minute! Watch out! I'll catch you!"

They ripped over the ground, hit the cookshack wall neck and neck, and collapsed in the dirt, breathless and giggling.

"Where'd your baby sister get a name like Princess Anne?" asked Manowar, sitting up and dusting off his knees.

"Don't you like it?"

"You bet I like it. Suits her to a tee. Only I never knew anybody else to have a name like that. How'd your folks happen to think of it?"

"They didn't," said Roosevelt. "I did."

"You did! How come?"

"Well, we were working in tomatoes, see, in Maryland, when she was born, and old Matthew, he said: 'Born in tomatoes. Let's name her Tomato!' Later on he said he'd only meant it for a joke, but it didn't sound like a joke to me. All I could see was how awful it would be for that little tyke to grow up with a name like Tomato, and here we were only a mile outside a town called Princess Anne. So I said, 'With a pretty name like Princess Anne right here waiting, why don't we call her Princess Anne?' And we did."

"Good boy," said Manowar. As he stood up, his

foot hit something. "Zowie! What's this?" he said.

"What'd you find?"

"Nothing but an old cherry-soda bottle. Empty."

Manowar stood up, started to toss away the bottle, and then drew back his arm. "Say!"

"Say what?"

"I can make something out of this. Watch. I'm going to make a present for Princess Anne." He rummaged in his pocket and pulled out a thick piece of rope three or four inches long. He stuffed one end of it into the neck of the bottle and then with care he frayed the other end till it was all fluffed out.

"Like cornsilk," said Roosevelt. "Like Mrs. Dinwiddie's hair. Neat!"

Manowar cradled the bottle on his arm and stroked the hair. "You think Princess Anne'll like it? Think she'll know it's a doll?"

"Yes, I do," said Roosevelt. "Come on." He jumped to his feet.

In the weeks since Quimby's Quarters Princess Anne had been growing fast. She made new sounds every day and you came to know usually what she meant by them, although she'd never yet made a sound you could really call a word. She hadn't ever

tried to walk, but with something to hang on to, she could pull herself to her feet and stand alone. She still used the washtub as her play pen; if she saw something outside it she wanted, she scrambled out, scooted off on her hands and knees to get what she was after, and then crawled back and climbed into the washtub again, happy as a clam.

When she saw the boys coming toward her, she began to shout. It sounded like a full sentence, only it didn't have any words in it.

"Hi, Princess. Remember me?" said Manowar. He knelt down beside the washtub. "Here. Here's a present for you." He rocked the bottle-doll back and forth in his hands and then handed it to her. She grabbed it, tugged at the hair and pulled the rope all the way out, raised the bottle high in the air and threw. It hit a stone and smashed into a hundred pieces.

Princess Anne shouted with glee. Then suddenly she stopped and set her lips tight together. She fastened her hands hard on the rim of the washtub. She opened her mouth.

"Ro-zee-vell," she said distinctly.

The Bust-out

It was Monday afternoon, the second week of school.

"Break it up, you two." Mamma called out the window. "Time to get going on dinner. Manowar, you want to eat with us? Chicken necks and rice and black-eyed peas?"

"Yes, ma'am!" said Manowar. He and Roosevelt sat side by side on the two cinder blocks that made a step from the Gradys' cabin door down to the ground.

"Come back in a little bit and it'll be ready. Roosevelt, will you go fetch me a bucket of water? Please?"

"Okay, Mamma. Right now." But Roosevelt didn't stir.

Manowar stood up. "You going to tell her?"

Roosevelt nodded. "Sure."

"Spunk. You got it."

"Not spunk. I got to tell her, that's all. The secret's half hers, and now there's three of us knows it."

"Will she be mad?"

"Maybe. Maybe not, when she knows I just busted out with it without meaning to. Specially when she knows it's you I told it to. She likes you."

"Going to tell her our plan?"

Roosevelt shook his head No, hard.

"No use to tell her that. We're the ones got to make it work. Suppose she said lay off. Then where'd we be?" Roosevelt leaned back into the doorway, reached an arm around inside for the bucket, stood up, and marched off to the community spigot.

His head churned. That place Manowar described sounded good, all right. Manowar had seen it, riding in Digger's bus. Digger got his crew lost once in a roundabout short cut through Macintosh County and there he saw the place. It was fruit country, all full of orchards and the trees right then in blossom, some white and some pink. Beside the road where the tire blew out, the blossoms were white. Pear trees, said the man who stopped to help with the tire.

And in that pear orchard there was this camp, made up of bus bodies in a line running straight back from the road exactly like a freight train. Set right down in the ground they were, wheels gone and nobody living in them because it wasn't fruit-picking time.

One bus—the fourth one back from the road—had a smoke pipe coming out the top and this couldn't mean more than one thing: a stove for keeping warm by in winter. Mamma always said there'd be something about the right place so they'd know it when they saw it. Maybe the something was that smoke pipe. Winters in the north are cold.

Manowar had looked into a window of this bus. Somebody had pulled out the seats and fixed walls across to make rooms, and he'd cut a little door into each wall for going to and fro. Mamma did say she wanted more than one room so she could go to and fro. It sounded great.

The trouble was, where exactly was it? And when they found out where it was, how could they get Cap Jackson to take them there? And when they got there, how could they get Papa to think Providence meant the Grady family should stay put there? He'd say no for sure unless there was work to do. How could you tell if there'd be work in the winter?

Roosevelt and Manowar had talked and talked about it and finally they'd figured out a plan. It might work or it might not, but anyway it was a starter. Only first Roosevelt had to tell Mamma about giving away their secret.

There wasn't anybody else around when he returned with the bucket of water except Princess Anne and she was asleep. So Roosevelt told it, fast, how he

hadn't meant to spill their secret but he got to talking to Manowar and out it busted.

He waited.

Mamma didn't say anything. Not anything at all. She made very busy lighting the oil stove and getting the chicken necks on to cook. Then she walked to the bed and sat down.

"You come here," she said.

Roosevelt went and stood in front of her. She took his hand.

"You did right to tell me," she said. "If you did right to let out our secret to Manowar, that I don't know, not yet I don't. But you didn't mean to tell, that I do know. So here's what you do. You let Manowar know we got a three-way secret now, me and you and him, and you tell him three for sure is enough people to know it. You tell him, hear?"

Roosevelt nodded. "I'll tell him. I like it to be a secret. But I was wondering . . ."

"Wondering what?"

"Why's it have to be a secret from Papa?"

"Did Manowar tell you to ask me that?" Mamma's voice was sharp.

"No, Mamma, no, no, he didn't. I thought of it myself. Only this minute I thought of it. It seems if Papa is looking for the place too, we'll find it faster. That's all."

Mamma looked out the window. Her words came slowly. She was thinking each one.

"Here's how it is, Roosevelt. Your papa can easy get his mind set against staying put and no matter how good a place we'd find, he might never do it. But if we creep up on him like and fix it so it looks to him as if Providence had it all set up, why then he'd like it fine. Understand?"

"I think so," said Roosevelt. "I certainly never thought of that. Mamma, you're smart. You're really smart."

"Not very. But I try." Mamma laughed, short. "Roosevelt, you like Manowar, don't you?"

"Yes, ma'am."

"So do I. Does he want a stay-put place, too?"

"I don't know. He never said. I never thought."

"Well, don't think. Just go and track down Sister and Matthew and get them to wash themselves before dinner. Scoot."

She gave him a kiss and a shove. He scooted.

The Plan

Manowar was long on thinking up things. He had ideas. Roosevelt was long on doing things in order. He liked system. They made a good team.

The plan they figured out had three steps to it. They had to take all three steps without letting anybody know what they were up to, even Mamma. That made it ticklish.

Step One: Find out the whereabouts of the bus camp.

Step Two: Figure out a way to get Cap Jackson to take his crew there.

Step Three: Hunt up a winter job for Papa.

"We know it's in Macintosh County," said Manowar. I'm almost certain of that. I'll ask Digger the name of the camp and what town it's near. He mostly knows all the camps in the state, and I never heard of another bus camp. He'll know which one I mean. I can ask him so he won't catch on. That way we'll lick Step One."

Next day in school, during lunch, Manowar reported.

"It's in Macintosh County, all right, up in the northwest corner. Elliott's Bus Camp, it's called, and it's three miles or so west of a town by the name of North Galilee. Digger wanted to know why I asked about it. I said I'd like to fix my teeth into one of those juicy ripe pears. He said no chance, Elliott charges rent for folks to live in his buses. Three dollars and fifty cents a week. Digger won't take his crew any place where they charge that kind of rent."

Roosevelt thought this sounded hopeful. He didn't know how Cap felt about taking his folks where there was that much rent to pay, but if Cap knew Digger wasn't going there, that would be one point in its favor. Cap would be happy if he never had to be in a camp again where Digger was.

On the other hand, it would be tough to pay three dollars and fifty cents a week rent all winter. And they had to eat, too. Papa would need a job for sure.

Right then Manowar had one of his ideas.

"About Step Three," he said, "we don't have to wait till Step Two is done to start on it. We could write a letter to this man Elliott who owns the bus camp and ask him about a winter job for your papa."

Roosevelt considered this. "If all he's got is pear trees, Mr. Elliott wouldn't have any winter jobs."

"Then how about writing to somebody else in North Galilee? Like a man in a gas station, maybe, who needs help selling gas?"

"We don't know the name of any man in a gas station."

"We could write to the mayor. Every town's got a mayor. He'd know everybody and everything. We don't have to know his name to write to him. There's only one mayor to a town, so he'd get the letter without any trouble. What can your papa do besides crops?"

"What kind of jobs would there be?"

"Oh, mailman, fireman, policeman, bus driver, sell things in stores, all like that. Can he fix cars?"

"I'm not sure. He knows everything about houses, though, dormer windows and attics and porches and such like. Down in Georgia once he worked in a sawmill."

"There! See? This will be easy."

But it wasn't easy. It took a whole day to get a letter written to suit them. Manowar's spelling was not the best, and Roosevelt's was only middling. They asked Mrs. Dinwiddie about some of the words they wanted to use but not too many for fear she'd get curious and ask questions about what they were doing. It took almost another day to decide who should sign the letter. Manowar thought Roosevelt should sign it. Roosevelt thought the secret would be safer if the answer came back to Manowar, so finally Manowar said all right, he'd sign it, what did he have to lose. This is what they wrote:

> Dear Mister Sir Mayer,
>   Will you have a winter job in North Galilee fireman policeman maleman bus driver sell gas or anything you got for sail or bild houses or work in a sawmil? Please anser quick.
>   Yours truly,
>   MANOWAR (MISTER)

Manowar licked the envelope.

"One thing I've been thinking," he said. "I know this began as a secret with your mother and you, but why keep it that way? Wouldn't it be a lot easier if your papa went looking for his own job his own self?"

"I know it looks that way, Manowar, but I told you. It has to stay a three-way secret. Here's how it is. Papa's not so fixed on staying put. If he thinks we and Mamma are pushing him into it, he's sure not to want to. He believes you should wait for Providence to have things ready."

"What's Providence?" asked Manowar.

"I don't rightly know, but it's something Papa sets store by. So we fix it for Papa to see a place and it looks right and there's a job there and everything, then he'll say to Mamma: 'Addie, it looks as if Providence is working our way. What do you say we stay here through a winter and find out?' He'll think Providence did the whole thing. See what I mean, Manowar?"

"Sure, I see. You're deep, you and your Mamma. Okay, we mail the letter."

They asked Mrs. Dinwiddie about getting a stamp and she sold them one out of her pocketbook. Each boy took two cents out of his lunch money to buy the stamp, and she made them a present of the odd penny. They posted the letter in the mailbox in front of the schoolhouse. That was Thursday.

The waiting was awful. Time slowed up again and came almost to a stop. It was hard to back up and think about Step Two when you were anxious about the answer to Step Three.

On Saturday Manowar said how about beginning Step Two by feeling out Cap Jackson on where he was thinking of going next. Talk about it easy-like, not making a big thing of it.

Roosevelt agreed. He watched his chance. Beans finished early that day, and somebody started a soft-ball game. Cap was watching the game when Roosevelt sauntered up to him. He waited for a lull in the game, then said, "Beans be over next week, Cap?"

"You worrying about school, Roosevelt? We'll stay through for the end of that, beans or no beans."

"Where do you figure we'll go next?"

"Fruit somewhere, most likely, up Macintosh County way. Some smaller camps up there. Early apples coming on soon. Potatoes, too, are close by, close enough for day hauls. Like to get our crew into some good camp ahead of the fruit-and-potato rush. I have a line on a couple of growers in Macintosh who want reliable crews like mine. Smith, he's tops to work for, but his camp smells. Johnson, he has an A-one camp, but he's a chiseler. I hear there's a fine man up that way who has a bus camp—very nice— only he charges too much rent. Three dollars and fifty cents a week for a family."

Roosevelt's heart hammered against his ribs. "Where's Digger going next?"

"You want we should go along with Digger so you won't lose your pal Manowar. Is that it? Roosevelt, I'd like to oblige, I really would, but wherever that Digger Burton takes his crew, I aim to head for a different place. Digger won't go to that bus camp, for sure. Too high-priced. Maybe I just might take my crew there, at that, if they have room for us and plenty of work so folks can afford the rent. Sorry about splitting up you and Manowar, but if my crew and Digger's spend too much time in the same camp, we're plain heading for trouble and there's no use in that. Trouble enough without looking for it. Well, son, we'll see."

Not till Tuesday did the answer come from the Mayor of North Galilee. It was the last week of school. Manowar hunted up Roosevelt before he opened the letter so they could read it together. Here's the way it went:

Dear Mr. Manowar:

We can always use a good fireman. We don't pay him anything, though. Our fire department is all volunteers.

The nearest we come to having a police-man is a justice of the peace and I'm it.

We have one postmaster and I'm it.

We use two men on rural delivery routes and

they're both healthy. So is the school bus driver.

If you want to come around at fruit-picking time, hunt me up. I raise pears mostly, but a few peaches and apples, too. Who knows? Something may turn up. Glad you wrote to me.

Yours truly,
JONATHAN ELLIOTT
Mayor of North Galilee

Manowar whistled.

"Elliott! And he raises pears. He's the bus camp man. And the mayor and the mailman and the policeman and everything. A big shot. Zowie!"

Roosevelt was not so excited. "I don't see this gets us very far. No promises."

"What did you expect? Man, this sounds super to me."

"What do we do next?"

"Looks to me, the big thing now is to get there. How sure are you of Cap?"

"Only middling sure. He said, 'We'll see.' That doesn't mean he's made his mind up."

"Then Cap's what we work on."

"That's right. But how?" Roosevelt sighed.

What more could they do without Cap's catching on? Nothing. Not anything at all. A long chance, that's what it was. Watch and wait. That's all they could do.

Roosevelt sighed again.

The Party

The idea of having a party did not begin until Wednesday, the day after Mr. Elliott's letter arrived. In two days more it would be Friday and that would be the last day of school. That morning Mrs. Dinwiddie pushed her sky-blue sweater sleeves up above her elbows and announced, "School ought to end with something special. Am I right?"

The class agreed. They talked it over and decided they would like to finish up with a party.

"What makes a party?" asked Mrs. Dinwiddie.

Company, the class told her. Food. Entertainment. And of course, surprises, wrapped up and tied with ribbons.

For company, they thought they would like to invite their parents, only if it rained, that is.

"Why only if it rains?" asked Mrs. Dinwiddie.

Lulubelle explained this. "If the sun shines, they'll be working in the fields."

"Of course," said Mrs. Dinwiddie. "Naturally. I forgot."

About food, maybe their parents would come to lunch if it rained.

"Wait till I talk to the principal," said Mrs. Dinwiddie. "He and I can figure something out." The principal, Roosevelt knew by this time, was the dressed-up man who'd stood in the cookshack door.

That noon Mrs. Dinwiddie sat for lunch with the principal and the other teachers at a table off by themselves.

The next thing the class knew, the Friday party had turned into a celebration for the whole school. All four classes. Every parent was to be invited, not for lunch, and depending on the weather, but for supper and come rain or shine.

About the surprises, Mrs. Dinwiddie was vague.

"Will they be wrapped up?" the class wanted to know.

"Not wrapped up, exactly," she told them, "but ribbons, yes. They'll be tied with ribbons."

After the party, after they were back home in their cabin that night, everybody in the Grady family had a different notion about what was the best feature of the celebration.

"The supper." That was Matthew's vote. "How can you beat spaghetti and ice cream? You tell me."

"The way Sister's class sang 'Good News, the Chariot's Coming.' That suited me fine," said Papa. "And that other song about 'A wall so high . . .' "

Sister picked up the words and sang them.

> ". . . so high, you can't go over,
> A wall so low, you can't go under,
> A wall so wide, you can't go round,
> You got to go in at the door."

"Everybody in dress-up clothes," she said. "That was the nicest." And she whirled round and round so her pink skirt flew up and showed her white ruffled petticoats—not one, not two, but three petticoats— all starched and ironed by Mamma between coming in from beans and time for the party.

"I liked all of it," Mamma said. "And best of everything, I believe, was Matthew's class saying the salute to the flag and ending up so plain and loud: 'It's great to be an American.' I liked that."

"The surprises. They were my favorite part," said Roosevelt, slipping the orange and black ribbons off

his certificate and unrolling the paper to look again
at what it said:

CENTRAL SCHOOL NUMBER SIX
Special Summer Session
This is to certify that
ROOSEVELT GRADY
completed three weeks of third-grade work
with distinction

The certificate was signed by the principal and
by Mrs. Dinwiddie: Joan Anderson Dinwiddie.
Roosevelt expected he'd keep that certificate a long
time—forever, probably. Inside his head, though,
was a piece of news that excited him even more.
He'd told it to Manowar while the party was breaking up. The two boys managed a hasty word together
over the drinking fountain as folks were milling
around and talking to the teachers and saying thank
you and good-by.

"Manowar. Guess what. We're going to Elliott's
Bus Camp!"

"For sure? How do you know?"

"I heard Cap tell it to Papa only a minute ago.
'Be ready at seven, Henry,' he said. 'Macintosh
County's a long ride, and Elliott's Bus Camp is way
up in the northwest corner. We need an early start.'
Those are exactly the words he said."

Manowar whistled. "Zowie! That's great. Now for Step Three."

"How about you? Where's Digger taking his crew?"

"He just told me. Smith's Camp, he's decided. Says the camp's a slum, but Smith has a lot of apples for picking and there's no rent to pay."

"Wish you were coming with us," said Roosevelt.

Manowar took an extra-long drink at the fountain before he spoke. "Eat a pear for me," he said. "And write me a letter, hear? Smith's Camp, Queen's Crossing, care of Digger Burton's crew. Tell me how Step Three comes out."

"I'll do that," Roosevelt promised.

Macintosh County

Elliott's Bus Camp looked to be precisely what Manowar had described, only more so. Every bus was painted gray with a neat red trim, and each one had electric lights and good cold water piped inside. No more carrying a bucket to some old community spigot.

Sixteen buses, there were: eight in a line running back from the road like a freight train, and then the line turned a corner and eight more buses ran along behind the pear orchard. Cap Jackson drove the full length of them in his truck just to see how many, and Roosevelt counted for him. Cap turned the truck around and drove back alongside the buses to the highway and everybody got out and walked around, looking and looking.

"See there, Papa," said Roosevelt. "The fourth

bus down has a smoke pipe coming out the roof. Ask if we can have that one? Please?"

"Why?" asked Papa. "Your mamma has an oil stove. What do we want with a smoke pipe?"

Right then Mamma put her word in. "We had a smoke pipe in Georgia, Henry, remember? On our house with the dog-run. I've been hoping always we'd find another house with a smoke pipe."

Papa laughed and said, all right, he'd see if they could get it. He saw, and they could, and they did.

When Mamma spotted those inside walls going across to make three rooms and a little door cut into each wall for going to and fro, she looked as if she might cry. This was scary.

"Don't you like it, Mamma?" Roosevelt was anxious.

"I like it fine, Roosevelt." She did halfway cry, but only one tear to each eye, and she wiped up each tear before it rolled out. "All I don't like is thinking about when the work runs out and we have to leave all this behind."

Pears were about over, but peaches and apples kept the Gradys busy. Some days the grown-ups went on long hauls into potato country.

The fourth bus down made a grand house. It was interesting to have three rooms for going to and fro in, but with working almost every day, Mamma was too

busy to do much about fixing things. Besides, know-ing they'd be moving when potatoes ended gave her no heart, she said, for spending evenings sewing and such.

Princess Anne kept on saying "Ro-zee-vell," but she showed no sign of trying any other words.

Sister missed Pearly Ann and took it out in moping. Even Matthew turned grumpy.

For Roosevelt, without Mrs. Dinwiddie and Manowar, all the zip was gone out of living. Time took to dragging the way it had those first two weeks at Willowbrook.

One day in August the ladies of North Galilee arrived at the bus camp with a thrift sale. What this meant was, a parade of cars drove in, each with two ladies in front and a bunch of old clothes on the back

seat. The camp manager set up sawhorses and planks for tables, and the ladies put out the clothes in piles. One lady took a hammer and a nail and tacked up a sign on a pear tree. The other ladies walked up and down beside the buses calling: "Thrift sale, thrift sale."

Pretty soon the people who weren't working swarmed out of their buses and began pawing at the clothes, joking and jostling each other and stirring up the heaps. Mostly the lookers were women, with here and there a man hunting himself a pair of shoes or some pants or a jacket.

Papa'd gone off early in the morning in Cap Jackson's truck fifty miles to potato country, but Mamma was there. She'd stayed home to catch up on wash and mending. She always enjoyed herself at thrift sales. She had a good eye for bargains, but as much as anything she liked the conversations with the ladies who came to sell.

Roosevelt and Sister hung around the edge of the crowd, doing the best they could to see what things people bought, but that wasn't good enough for Matthew. Somehow or other he managed to wriggle in between folks and right up front to the table. It was no time before he'd latched on to a dark blue coat with brass buttons and when a woman wanted to look at it, he wouldn't let go.

One of the selling ladies saw right away that Mamma knew good stuff from trash. "You looking for something special?" she said. "Maybe I can help."

"Sweaters, I think," said Mamma. "For the children. We look to stay here through potatoes, and come late September, sweaters will feel good."

The lady let Mamma carry a bunch of clothes off to a clear space under a pear tree so the children could try them on. They ended up with something for everybody: a sky-blue sweater like Mrs. Dinwiddie's for Sister; the dark blue coat with the brass buttons for Matthew; for Roosevelt, a bright green sweater that looked to be the exact same color as Manowar's corduroy jacket. And for Princess Anne, a cute pink coat with white fur trimming around the neck and down the front and all the way around the bottom. Everything was twenty-five cents apiece except Princess Anne's coat. It cost fifty cents—all that fur.

"How about something for yourself?" the lady asked Mamma.

"I think not," said Mamma. "Not unless I see just the thing. What's that over there? That heap of dark red?"

"That's some velvet drapes. At least they used to be drapes in my living room. Last year I made them into stage curtains for a play we had in Sunday school. The church made enough money on the play to buy new stage curtains, and I must have put these old ones in my attic. Anyway, that's where I found them yesterday and I thought I'd bring them along here. There might be somebody who'd like them. They're nice material, only a little faded here and there in streaks where the sun hit them. A body could cut out the faded streaks and put the rest to all kinds of use."

She pushed the pile over and lifted up a corner of it for Mamma to feel.

"It's a lovely color," said Mamma, stroking with one finger, "and so soft."

"You can have the whole thing for a dollar," the lady told her. "It's four pairs stitched together, floor length, and I wouldn't dare say to you what I paid for them new."

"A dollar," said Mamma. She held up a length and

put her head on one side and looked. "It'd be a bulk to tote around the country, but I do like the color and the feel."

"Seeing you bought all those sweaters," said the lady, "I'll make it seventy-five cents."

Mamma thought a minute.

"I'll take it," she said.

"What's it for?" asked Matthew. "What are you going to do with it?"

"Not anything this minute," Mamma told him. "Maybe not anything for a long time, but it suits me and if I buy it now, it'll be ready when I have a need. And there's no call for you to talk about this. If I'd rather have it than a dress, that's my business. Hear?" And that was every word she'd say about the matter.

She paid for the velvet and gathered it up. It filled her arms full right up to her chin.

"Roosevelt, you bring along the other things. Please?"

By the time Roosevelt had gathered up the sweaters and coats and carried them inside their bus, the dark red velvet was out of sight.

Roosevelt wandered outside again. The piles on the table had dwindled to plain rubbish and the crowd was thinning out. His eyes fixed themselves on the sign tacked on the pear tree. He read it over, every word:

THRIFT SALE
For the Benefit of the
North Galilee Library
Everybody Welcome

Library. A place full of books. Mrs. Dinwiddie
had explained how a library works. They give you a
card with your name on it and they let you borrow
books and take them home and read them. You have
to carry them back on time or you pay a fine.
Roosevelt thought he'd like to have a book to read.
The sign said, "Everybody Welcome." Maybe they'd
have that book with Manowar's favorite story in it,
the one about the baby standing on its head.

He walked up to the lady who'd waited on his
mother and tugged at her arm.

"Please, ma'am," he said.

She was busy making change. When she finished,
he tugged again.

"Please, ma'am," he said, "about the library.
There's a book I want to read. Please, will you give
me a card? With my name on it?"

The lady looked at him blankly. You'd think she'd
never seen him before.

"A card? Oh, you mean a library card. I haven't
any. You'd have to go to the library to get one." She
looked doubtful. "I'm afraid the library is for the

people in North Galilee. The residents. The ones who belong."

"Oh," said Roosevelt. "I see." That again. Residents. The ones who belong.

He looked down. His big toe found a little hole in the ground. He screwed his toe around in it to make it deeper. Then with the side of his foot he pushed the dirt back in and stepped on it and smoothed it over till you'd never guess there'd been a hole there at all. For a minute he stood stock still. All at once he turned his back on the selling lady and the thrift sale and everything and he made for the Grady bus. It was empty. On through the two inside doors he went and into the room he shared with Matthew. He rummaged around and found a pencil and a piece of paper. He sat down on the floor and wrote:

Dear Manowar,

The forth bus down is ours smoke pipe and all and we like it fine only no stove but I gess we move on anyway when apples and potatoes run out becaus I cant figure how to do about Step Three. Too bad you arent hear we mite think of something.

Take it eazy man

Your friend

ROOSEVELT GRADY

P.S. I have a thrift sale swetter. Green like your jakett. Princess Annes is pink and got white furr triming.

Step Three

September brought Labor Day, and it was a day Roosevelt never forgot.

There was no mail delivery because it was a holiday, but Mr. Elliott, being the postmaster, brought the mail on Sundays and holidays and left it in the first bus, which was the camp manager's office.

Early that morning Roosevelt walked up to the first bus to see if he might have a letter from Manowar. Mr. Elliott himself was there with the mail. It was the first time Roosevelt had spoken to him or even seen him close up. He was a big man with snappy eyes and quite a lot of hair, white, and a mustache and eyebrows to match.

"Grady, you say?" Mr. Elliott thumbed through the letters. "No. Nothing here for Grady. Grady! Why, you must be the son of the man who spoke to me about the job in the fertilizer plant."

Roosevelt's breath caught.

"Fact is, you look like him. Henry Grady. Is he your father?"

Roosevelt nodded.

"Tell him I talked to the foreman over at the plant and he says there'll be a spell of work there, come winter. Not three months steady the way your father wanted, but more than a little spell and more than one spell, too. Enough to see you folks through the winter, all right, and on into spring. Tell your father I'll be around in a little bit to talk about it."

Roosevelt tried to say yes, sir or thank you or something polite like that, but the words stuck. All he could do was make a little bow and back out of the bus and tear home. Running with his head down, he catapulted smack into Papa.

"Whoa," said Papa, catching him. "What's the rush?"

As soon as Roosevelt fetched back his breath, he explained. "The fertilizer plant. Mr. Elliott said I should tell you. Said he'd be around to talk to you about it. Not three months steady, but spells enough to carry us through to spring. So we can stay here. Can't we? Please? Please?"

"Elliott saying that, yes, it looks as if we might. Yes, it does. We'll see what your mamma says."

"She'll say Yes. I know she'll say Yes. She's a-bound to. You'll see."

Hand in hand, they walked along toward the fourth bus down.

"Papa?"

"What, son?"

"What made you think about the fertilizer plant? What made you not wait for Providence? Why'd you ask about three months work? Just three months?"

Papa didn't answer right away. When they came to the door, he pushed Roosevelt in first and then he put a hand on his shoulder and turned him around. Standing in the doorway made Roosevelt almost tall enough to look straight into Papa's eyes. Not quite, but nearly.

"Roosevelt, do you remember back in the spring that time you were sick?" Roosevelt nodded. "Remember what that doctor said to Mamma about Matthew's foot?" Roosevelt nodded again. "Remember how long he said it would take him to find out if he could mend it?"

Roosevelt's eyes widened. "Oh, Papa! That's why you told Mr. Elliott three months. And now we'll have all winter. Oh, Papa, can we? Can we find a doctor? Can we get his foot fixed by spring?"

"Hush. I don't know. Don't get your mamma excited. I don't know if we can get it fixed at all. It'll take time to find out, and it'll take something else we don't have. Money. Now it looks as if we'll have the time and we'll have to figure about the money. I've been looking first to see a place we could be sure of staying in long enough for some doctor to try about the foot. When we drove in here that day from Willowbrook, remember I was riding in front with Cap Jackson? There by the edge of town, something made me turn my head and look to the right, and there sat that red brick building with the white letters painted on the wall: 'North Galilee Fertilizer Company.' Right then I figured I was meant to have a shot at a job there."

"Papa? What was it made you turn your head to the right? Was it Providence?"

"I reckon it was, Roosevelt. Yes, I reckon it was. Addie!" he called. "Addie! Where are you?"

Sister answered. "She's over visiting Mrs. Jackson, Papa."

Papa started away toward the Jackson's bus. He'd taken hardly one step when he called back over his shoulder: "Roosevelt! Roosevelt, you want to see Providence operating, you come to the door and turn your head to the right." He laughed and walked on.

Roosevelt poked his head out the door and looked to the right. Off there up by the highway who ever should be loping toward him but Manowar. When he saw Roosevelt, he began to run. Providence was working, for sure. Manowar had on his green corduroy jacket, and swinging from one finger by a string was his red-and-white bundle of treasures. Roosevelt ran to meet him.

"Zowie," said Manowar. "I got your letter and this is the first day Digger's let me loose." He laughed. "He didn't exactly let me loose today, but here I am."

"How'd you get here?" asked Roosevelt.

"There's a bus comes along from Smith's Camp to here. Only takes a couple of hours. I purely had to come and see if there isn't something we can figure to do about Step Three."

"Step Three is fixed!"

Barely had Roosevelt finished telling the news about the North Galilee Fertilizer Company when along came Mr. Elliott, hugging to his stomach a cute little potbellied iron stove.

"There," he said, resting the stove on the ground and puffing. "Heavy. Glad to set it down. You folks look to stay through the winter, you'll need this. Nobody yet has stayed in one of these buses all through to spring, but that's no reason you shouldn't try. One man thought to stay and that's why I put the chimney in. Along about Thanksgiving time, though, his feet got cold and he lit out. You'll need a shovel, too, to get you out to the highway. We get snowbanks. Who's your friend?"

Roosevelt swallowed and found his voice was working.

"Manowar. He's come to visit me. His name's Manowar." The minute he said the name a second time, he remembered something. His heart took a flip. It was Manowar who'd signed their letter to the mayor. What would Mr. Elliott think?

"Well, well. Manowar, is it? Shake."

Mr. Elliott put out his hand. Manowar shook it.

"So you're Mister Manowar. I've been wondering when you'd show up. Wondered what you'd look like, too. That was quite a letter you wrote me. I figured you'd be a few sizes larger than you are. Got a job yet?"

"No, sir," said Manowar. "That is, I've been a handy-boy for a crew leader over at Smith's Camp."

"Have been, you say? Aren't you now?"

Manowar kept his eyes away from Roosevelt and looked straight at Mr. Elliott. "No, sir."

"Why not?"

"I quit."

"When?"

"Last night."

"Why?"

"Just, I quit. That's all."

"Who was the crew leader?"

"Digger Burton."

"Digger Burton! That slippery operator? I know him from way back. Brought his roistery crew to my place one summer and we really had a ruckus. He had a lot of fancy ways to collect money from them

and me too. Crooked as a corkscrew. I fired him out
of my camp. Wouldn't have him around again at
any price. No wonder you quit. Congratulations.
What are your plans?"

"He's going to visit me," said Roosevelt.

"Your mother know about this?"

"No, sir, but she won't mind. She'll be glad. She
likes Manowar."

"How do you know she likes him?"

"She said so."

"Oh, she did, did she?" He smoothed his mustache
in both directions. "One good thing, Manowar can
earn his keep while he's visiting. I plan to push up a
couple of old pear trees around here and he'll be
doing me a favor to chop them up for the Gradys to
burn in that potbellied stove."

He looked at his watch.

"I have to run. Promised to ride my horse in the
North Galilee Labor Day parade. Better come and
see how I do. Get Cap Jackson to put you in his truck
and bring you. Other folks, too. Everybody welcome.
About an hour from now, the band plays and we'll be
lined up to begin. So long, men."

He stepped off toward the highway.

"So long," called the boys, sounding like one voice.
They stood there looking at each other and grinning,
neither one saying a word. At last:

"Manowar, this is super," said Roosevelt. "How'd
you come to quit Digger?"

"I'll show you." Manowar knelt on the ground and untied his red-and-white bundle. He spread out his treasures.

"Look."

There they were, the star, the petrified wood, the book, the necklace—and the applewood horse in two pieces, his head, and the rest of him, broken right off at the neck in the middle of his curly mane.

"O-o-o-o-h," gasped Roosevelt. "How awful. Did Digger do that?"

Manowar nodded. "Last night, in one of his mean spells. At Smith's place—it's a slum, all right, an old barn, but I drew a sort of a stall, all mine, with a crib at one end where they used to feed the horse. That crib made a dandy place to examine my treasures. I was in there looking them over when Digger came in. He walked right up to the crib and stood beside me.

" 'What's all this junk?' he said. 'You been holding out on me?' He made a grab for the squash blossoms, but I got there first. I swept up the kerchief and everything and ducked out under his arm. Only the little horse dropped out. Digger picked it up and threw it after me. I raced outside and hid in a ditch. He came out calling and calling, but he couldn't find me. So when I was sure he'd given up and gone, I slunk back in and found my little horse on the floor, lying there without any head. I looked and looked about an hour, and finally, way over in a corner, there was the head."

Manowar gathered up his treasures.

"Let me look at that horse," said Roosevelt. He held the body and the head together and kept turning them different ways until he found how they fitted. He held them tight together and all you could see wrong was the crack around the neck.

"There's hardly a thing my papa can't mend," he said. "You'll be surprised what he can mend. You let me give these pieces to him. He can fix them so you'd hardly guess they were ever broken."

"You think so?"

"Yes, I do. I'm just about certain," said Roosevelt.

Up by the first bus an automobile horn went *honkety-honk*. The boys looked up and there was Mr. Elliott leaning out the window of his car and beckoning. The boys ran up to him.

"Almost forgot," said Mr. Elliott. "Here's something I meant to tell your parents and now I'll tell it to you. Beginning tomorrow morning, Tuesday, ten minutes before eight, the school bus comes by here on the highway. You got some brothers and sisters?"

"Yes, sir," said Roosevelt. "Two, the right size for school."

"Get them scrubbed up and ready and yourselves, too. Ten minutes ahead of eight o'clock—mind you, ahead of eight o'clock—not after. That's when the school bus stops here. You be on hand. Both of you."

"Me, too?" asked Manowar.

"Of course, you too. This is one of my jobs your letter didn't ask about, Manowar. School board. I aim to keep the school bus full. Round up all the prospects."

"You mean," asked Roosevelt, "we get to go in the regular school bus? To the regular school? Right along with the residents? With everybody who belongs?"

"Why not?" And Mr. Elliott slapped his right foot down on the gas pedal and the car shot to the edge of the highway. There he braked it and looked both ways.

"So long for now," he called. "See you at the Labor Day parade." And off roared the car into the highway and up the hill toward North Galilee.

Nobody could understand why Mamma wouldn't go to the Labor Day parade.

"Don't you want to hear the band play?" Sister asked her. "And watch Mr. Elliott ride his horse?"

"It's just there's something I want to do that's more important," was all Mamma'd answer.

Matthew was shocked. "There's nothing more important than the North Galilee Labor Day parade. There couldn't be!"

"More important to me, I mean to say," said Mamma.

"Won't it keep, Addie?" Papa asked.

Mamma smiled at him. It was a beautiful smile. "Yes, Henry, it would keep. But *I* wouldn't. I plain have to get it going this minute or bust from joy."

So everybody clambered into Cap Jackson's truck, everybody that is, but Mamma. When Cap ground the starter, Roosevelt hung over the tailgate to wave good-by to her, but she'd already gone into the Grady bus. He could see her inside, but she never saw him. She didn't even look. She was busy holding the red velvet up to the first window, measuring where to cut for size.